The American Heir

A Jet City Billionaire Serial Romance

Gina Robinson

Three Jays Press LLC
SEATTLE, WASHINGTON

www.ginarobinson.com

Book Layout ©2013 BookDesignTemplates.com
Cover Design by Jeff Robinson

The American Heir, The Billionaire Duke Series/Gina Robinson. —
1st ed.
ISBN 978-0692731239

THE AGENT EX SERIES
"Full of laughter, intrigue, and, of course, steamy spies." —*RT Book Reviews*

CHAPTER ONE

Witham House, England
Riggins Feldhem, Duke of Witham

I never knew looks could kill in so many pointed ways. Until that moment. Each one I received from the instant I watched the damned entertainment news and stepped from the car until the last one on Haley's face as I confronted her in our bedroom pierced my heart from a different angle.

The smug, gleeful look of carnage on the TV show host's face as she read the teleprompter: "Haley, Duchess of Witham, is pregnant, a close friend of the duchess revealed exclusively to *Entertainment Britain*. It's not official yet, but expect an announcement from the duke and duchess soon..."

Not official? Hell. The purported father was as surprised as anyone. *I* hadn't heard it from the duchess' lips. If there was any news to be heard.

Denial is always the first stage of grief. *No. Haley wouldn't. She couldn't be. She wouldn't trick me. She would have told me. It's the fucking tabloids again making things up to sell a story. Trying to be salacious.*

Though my mind couldn't quite make out why a woman having her husband's baby was sensational. Unless you knew the truth of our situation.

The look on the face of the driver as he opened the car door in the driveway of my home, my literal castle. If a man's home was truly his castle, mine felt at that moment more like a dungeon. The driver's expression clearly said, in its British way, *Poor sod. He's been played for a chump.*

But what did he know? Certainly not the unconventional details of my marriage.

Gibson's was the worst. Or maybe it was mine, if I could have seen it. I would have, if I'd bothered to look in any handy polished surface, which abounded. I avoided it for good reason. I didn't need to see the thunder and shock I already felt.

Gibson's was positively stoic as he opened the castle door to let its returning duke in. "Your Grace. We weren't expecting you back—"

"No?" With roses and lingerie in hand, I felt ragged, searching. I wanted the truth, damn it. Not gossip. And unfortunately, I was finding the ugly truth bit by bit. "I should have let you know I was coming. My apologies,

Gibson. I wanted to surprise the duchess. Is she at home?"

She damn well better be at this hour of night.

He nodded. "She's in her room, sir. She's been staying in the duchess' suite since shortly after you left. In Helen's old room. You'll find her there."

"She's been feeling poorly?" I tried to keep the hardness and inquisition out of my voice. Despite my best efforts, I hardly sounded casual. Or sympathetically worried. And definitely not friendly.

"I couldn't say, sir." Gibson was hedging.

I cursed beneath my breath. His allegiance had clearly shifted to the duchess. He was *my* employee. He was supposed to be loyal to *me*.

"More tired than usual?"

"Running this estate would wear anyone out, sir." He laughed as if he'd made a small joke.

There was no humor in me.

"Has she thrown up in any of my priceless vases lately, as the news is claiming? Or even any of my cheap ones?" I pronounced vase in the British way, without the long A and definite S.

Gibson clearly knew what I was referring to. "I'm not aware that you own *any* cheap vases, sir."

Gibson wouldn't give up with the attempt to divert me. Nor did he seem inclined to make even a feeble stab at allaying my concerns. He wouldn't be caught in the middle of a domestic crisis. Smart man.

Maybe he was right. Maybe there was nothing to worry about. I half expected him to tell me not to listen to tittle-tattle. He wisely refrained.

I nodded to Gibson and took the stairs two at a time with the bouquet and gift box bobbing in my hands, trying to calm my nerves. Innocent until proven guilty, that was the American way, wasn't it? Hadn't I been a victim of gossip often enough to know not to listen to it, let alone believe it?

I was going to go ahead with my plan. Tell her I loved her. Laugh with her about the things the press made up. Things would be better than they were before. I loved her. I had to tell her. That was the important thing.

Until I threw open the bedroom door and found her sitting in bed watching TV, with a Bible, of all things, next to her. And a tube of digestive biscuits.

Crackers in bed? Damn it. Damn it all. How terribly clichéd. All she needed was a jar of pickles and a quart of ice cream to complete the picture.

With her silvery hair slipping over her shoulders, she looked as pale as milk glass. I knew every inch of her body. I'd memorized it before I left and replayed the beauty of it in my mind over and over since. I ran my gaze over her, meticulous in my study. Already her breasts looked fuller and lush with impending motherhood.

My gut tightened. My heart was gripped in a vise of tangled emotions. My hands shook. I went cold.

The words of the newscast haunted me. *The duchess is already experiencing morning sickness and reportedly retched into a priceless antique vase during a friend's very recent visit...*

I asked the question I didn't want answered. "Is it true? Are you pregnant?"

I hadn't thought it was possible for her to go any paler, but she lost all color, going so completely white her skin was almost translucent.

I'd been wrong. The look on her face was the worst look of all. It pierced my heart straight on and straight through. She didn't even have to speak. Her expression was more than enough.

We stood staring at each other, frozen in time. Frozen in emotion. Each waiting for the other to make a move.

She tossed back the covers and slid off the bed. For an instant, I thought, I hoped, I prayed, she was coming to me. That she was running to me to throw her arms around me and take me to her. Despite my outward confidence, I was an insecure guy. I wanted unconditional love, desperately.

She brushed past me almost defiantly, threw open the door, and ran into the bathroom. The door shook and rattled, and bounced on the doorstop behind her. The sound of the porcelain toilet lid banging open followed. Next the violence of throwing up, that horrific vomiting noise that brought the bile to my throat. I fought back my gag response.

Anger. Pain. Frustration. A toxic cocktail raged inside me. I dropped the package on the dresser and smashed the bouquet against the wall with all my might. Whipping the wall with it. Lashing out. Lashing anything. Again and again. Until the red petals spilled onto the floor like the blood of our relationship.

"Bloody, bloody hell!" I yelled, resorting to British curses.

I kicked the baseboard, fighting rage and hurt. When my anger was finally spent, I leaned my forehead against the wall, trying to process the shock and betrayal. *Calm down, man. Just fucking calm down.*

The sound of vomiting continued, more violent than it had been.

I could be a hard man at times. But I never could stand seeing other people in pain. Hearing Haley losing her digestive biscuits with such violence was almost more than I could bear.

I dropped the battered roses and went into the bathroom. Haley kneeled in front of the toilet, pitifully trying to hold her hair out of the way as she leaned over the bowl.

Despite the rage coursing through me, I gently took her hair from her and held it back until, clutching her stomach, she broke into dry heaves, took a shaky breath, and sat up straight on her knees. She was still as white as if she'd seen our patron ghost in the Ghost Tower. Sweat beaded on her forehead and nose. Even her lips were eerily pale blue.

I dropped her hair and ran her a glass of water. My hand shook as I held it out to her. "I take it this isn't the stomach flu." It would have been an innocuous enough statement, if it hadn't been laced with the venom of my hurt and anger.

She took the water and rinsed her mouth. But to my surprise, her eyes were hard and fierce when she turned them back on me. "Congratulations. You're going to be a papa." She emphasized the second syllable of "papa" in the British way, almost making it sound elegant rather than lower class and antiquated.

Her words would have been innocent, too, even cele-bratory, if her eyes hadn't been snapping with that old throwing-daggers look. I hadn't expected venom from her. Triumph, maybe. Joy, possibly. My heart stopped.

The look on her face killed everything, including the words on my lips and the happiness of knowing I loved her. That look nearly killed me.

"Bloody hell, duke!" The rancor of her words rever-berated off the porcelain toilet. "What are you doing here?"

"I wanted to surprise you." There was no love in my voice.

Her voice broke. "How long have you known?"

I frowned. "That you're pregnant?" I hitched my thumb, indicating the great outdoors and the circular drive below our window. "Since about five minutes ago in the car."

"Don't play dumb with me."

I'd never heard her sound so angry. She was a dif-ferent person. Under other circumstances, I would have offered her a Snickers, hoping it would turn her back into herself and lighten the mood. Even though she'd just tossed her cookies, hunger wasn't why she wasn't herself.

"What are you talking about?" I was supposed to be the one who was upset here. I was the one who'd been trapped into fatherhood. I had the right to be indignant, not her. Did she not want this baby either? Did that make me feel better? Or worse?

"How long have you known that the Dead Duke is my great-grandfather, not my great-something uncle by marriage?" She wiped her mouth with a piece of toilet paper, looking up at me both beautiful and terrible.

My mouth went dry. My head spun.

"The DNA test," she said. "My unusual results? Were you comparing my DNA to the Dead Duke's? Is that what took so long?"

My mind stumbled. "You asked not to tell you the results," I said, confused. And still edgy and angry. "You begged me not to tell you—"

"I"—she tapped her chest—"*I* am the rightful duchess. The rightful heir to this dukedom. Not just the great-great-niece of a former duchess. But the direct descendant of the *duke*. *I* am the American heir.

"It's all spelled out in that letter I found in the Dead Duke's mother's Bible. When were you going to tell me? Ever?"

My hands shook. "I don't know what the hell you're talking about." I pointed to myself. "I'm the rightful heir of this place. *Me.* And no one else."

She cupped her still flat abdomen. "And this baby."

I glared at her. "Only if it's a boy." I turned on my heel and took a step toward the door.

"Troglodyte!" she screamed at me. "A girl may not be able to be duke. But she can inherit this estate. She *will* inherit this estate. The entailment is broken, Riggins. You can leave the estate to whomever you want. And it damn well better be this baby!"

I stormed out, shaking with rage and hurt. Ignoring the shattered rose petals and the gift box of diamond lingerie I'd left on the dresser. I raged all the way to the master suite, the lord of the castle's room, and banged the door shut so hard I swore the whole castle shook.

I collapsed on the bed, elbows on my knees, head in my hand. *What the fuck am I going to do now?*

CHAPTER TWO

Haley

I let Riggins go. Just let him walk. While I sat on the floor, trembling, leaning against the toilet bowl, trying to calm my stomach and my nerves. *Clutching a toilet for support.* This had to be a new low. Damn him. *Just damn him.*

I blinked back as many tears as I could and wiped the ones that escaped with the back of my hand. I'd gone on the attack intentionally.

I *was* angry with him. And my feelings *were* hurt. Which fueled my wrath and made it easier to lash out. But more than that, I couldn't let him say that he didn't want this baby. I couldn't. I *wouldn't*. There were things he'd never be able to unsay. Accusations that could never be rescinded. Lines I couldn't bear for him to cross.

Bounds he'd never forgive *himself* for stepping over.

Oh, I wasn't stupid or blind. I knew what he was thinking. It had been written plainly on his face. He thought I'd tricked him into marriage by pretending to comply with his wishes and gotten pregnant on purpose to get my hands on more millions. To make a land grab for the estate I was so clearly completely in love with. That I had schemed to be the dowager duchess and mother of a future duke forever. To gain control of a generous trust fund and have lasting influence over the estate for my lifetime.

He gave me more credit for cunning than I probably deserved. I was many things. But conniving generally wasn't one of them.

But he thought all of these things, and probably more, in the black, curling smoke of his dark thoughts. Thoughts that blinded him to the joy. To the solution to his problems.

He was too angry and hurt right now to see reason. And I was too weak to make him. Or even try to convince him.

It was one thing not being naïve. One thing to know he was thinking these things. But a completely different situation to hear him voice them. To have him hurl them at me with the venom of his shock poisoning his reason, words, and emotions.

It would break my heart irreparably if he said them aloud. Eventually, it would break his, too. And it would break us apart.

There were very few things I was certain of in this world. But among them were these—my baby would have a present and active father. Riggins wasn't going to abandon this baby. Not as long as I had breath in my body. And I wasn't going to abandon my family ancestry. I wouldn't let the Feldhem legacy die. I was a Feldhem. A real, *true* Feldhem. Feldhems had held this land for centuries. I wouldn't be the duchess who let it go. And Riggins wouldn't be that duke, either.

I was going to have my duke, my baby, and Sid was going to be cured. I wasn't giving up on any of it. We were all going to live happily ever after if it killed me.

I stood up shakily and leaned against the bathroom counter. Riggins had come home to surprise me. That gave me hope. I had to believe whatever had driven him here hadn't been murdered by this temporary setback.

My parents dying when I was young. Sid's health problems. All the tragedies of my life had made me tough. Made me a fighter. Molded me into an eternal optimist. What alternative did I have?

I felt weak as I made my way into the bedroom and discovered red rose petals littering the carpet just inside the bedroom. The smashed remains, bare stems now, forlornly wrapped in florist's paper, lay on the dresser next to a prettily wrapped gift box from an expensive lingerie store in Seattle.

I ignored the dead roses, grabbed the box, which was surprisingly heavy for lingerie, and lifted the lid. Inside, the gift was wrapped in pink tissue and sealed with a gold embossed sticker. I peeled the sticker away, pulled back the tissue, and gasped. Sparkling back at me was the sexiest jeweled bra I'd ever seen and a tiny pair of matching thong panties. I wasn't going to fit in these for long. I suddenly regretted the pregnancy only in the sense these lovely things deserved to be worn often.

I pulled the bra from the box and held it to the light, where it sparkled like the crown jewels. It was heavy, and covered in what were either real gemstones and diamonds, or very good-quality crystals. I wasn't a trained eye, but I voted for real. Short of the Neiman Marcus catalog or the annual Victoria's Secret diamond fantasy bra, I had never seen anything like them. Certainly not in person.

"Oh, Riggins," I whispered with tears in my eyes. "What does this mean?"

My heart was breaking, yet filled with hope. These had to be worth millions. Even the bra straps were covered with diamonds. Damn Rose. I wouldn't let her win.

I would wear these beautiful things for Riggins and win his heart. I carried the jeweled lingerie to the bed, where I should have been wearing them and making love with Riggins. I set them gently on the bed next to me. I was overwhelmed with emotion and new discoveries.

To my relief, the letter from Clara Wares White, the woman who was supposedly my great-grandmother, to Rans, the Duke of Witham, was still on the bed. I hadn't thought Riggins had time to grab it. But I had a moment of panic that he had. That he'd been angry enough to grab and destroy it. Believe it or

not, it was as precious to me as the glittering underwear in the box next to me.

I grabbed my cell phone and snapped a picture of
the letter and emailed it to myself. Just in case I ever
needed proof. Then I saved a copy to my online cloud
storage. That's how determined I was not to lose it.

I took a deep breath, gently smoothed the letter out,
and read it again. Slowly this time. Trying to understand. Letting myself be transported back in time to
another era. To a time when an unwed mother was
shamed and the baby punished for the sins of its parents.

Dearest Brother-in-law, dear Rans,

*It appears you're going to outlive us all after all. It
must be your steady English blood and stiff upper lip
that keeps you going. God knows you've endured
enough heartache to kill several men of less hearty con-
stitution.*

*I'm dying, Rans. Quickly, I hope. I have an aggres-
sive form of cancer that we caught late. I will be dead
by the time you read this letter, per my wishes. My
lawyer has instructions to mail it only after I'm gone.
Very dramatic, isn't it? Like something out of a novel.*

*But I rather enjoy being dramatic at my age. There
isn't much more to live for or much fun to be derived
from anything except what's in my mind. Anyway,
there is a point to this letter. A reason I'm writing you
on my deathbed. I made a promise to my sister, your
beloved Helen, many years ago. The time has come to
make good on it. I thank God my mind is still clear and*

sound enough to remember the promises I made in my youth.

Maybe this will give you some comfort. In any case, I hope you won't blame Helen. That this won't sully your memory of her or diminish your epic love. I can't think of any way to tell you this but straight out and then explain.

My daughter Gloria is adopted. She's your daughter. Yours and Helen's. Congratulations, you have a girl, old bean!

And now you have a new baby great-granddaughter, too. Just born. Has the Wares good looks, fortunately.

What you do with this information is up to you, of course. I'll be gone and unable to interfere with whatever you choose to do. I would ask that you respect them. My granddaughter is happily married, happily middle class, happily American. Please don't upset her life.

Now that I've dumped this on you in my final hours, I owe you the particulars. You always were one for details.

You broke Helen's heart all those years ago when she went to England the first time. It's still hard for me to believe Papa sent her to England to catch a member of the aristocracy. He was hoping for as much as an earl, I'm sure. That she landed a duke, or so it seemed, was beyond his wildest expectations.

My sister was always a romantic, a follower of her heart, a lover of passion, a giver. Easily seduced, as you well know. Easily hurt. But headstrong and just plain strong, period. You made love to her. Made her fall in love with you. When she realized you wanted her only for her money, not herself, she came home broken. You never saw that part. The hurt little girl, her rosy view of the world and romantic love shattered.

She hadn't been home long when she became listless. She looked pale. Wouldn't eat. Lost weight. Slept all the time. Papa and Mama thought she was depressed and spent their hours trying to cheer her up. Only I saw through it. Maybe trying so desperately to get pregnant all those years made me keen to recognize the symptoms of pregnancy when everyone else was blind.

Helen knew, though. And was terrified. What was she going to do? She'd disgraced the family. Papa would be devastated. Ruined. His health had already begun to fail. I, on the other hand, had come to terms with being barren. Now I saw my opportunity. I wanted the baby. I made my case to Helen. We both agreed it was for the best, the perfect solution for everyone.

We cooked up a plan and sent Helen away to New York and the East to "cheer her up" and mend her broken heart. She was gone a long time. Over nine months. In the meantime, I made plans to adopt a baby from a "friend" who was in trouble.

It all worked out. We were exceedingly careful and clever. But I'm still amazed we were never caught or found out. You were the one fly in the ointment. All those damned letters of yours that began arriving with a fury. There were times, many of them, when I thought Helen would relent and open one.

Would you hate me very much if I told you I encouraged her not to? You must understand. I wanted that baby with my heart and soul. With every ounce of my being. What right did you have to her?

But no force on earth could make Helen do something she didn't want to. And she was too hurt to want to hear from you. She had the baby, my beloved Gloria. Who was truly my daughter. I have loved her as my own and cherished her all my life. She has been my greatest gift. Her and her daughter and now her granddaughter. I hope that's some comfort. Though maybe my confession will only make you jealous and angrier.

Bygones, Rans. It was a bygone era. It's now a bygone life. For me, anyway. You'll probably live to be a hundred. What would you have done with a daughter? She wouldn't have been the precious male heir you so badly needed. But I have loved her.

Anyway, back to Helen. We got lucky. She popped back into shape and good spirits, seemingly none the worse for the wear, as they say. No stretch marks. No scars. After she gave Gloria to me, the baby was my daughter. She was her auntie. Helen never looked back. And neither should you.

Mama and Papa were thrilled to have their sunny daughter back. And then you showed up to reclaim Helen. You with your Clark Gable good looks and your English charm and title—how could she resist you? Especially when you were finally determined to have her. You have always been a force to be reckoned with. Damn your charm, Rans. You took my sister away.

I don't think you ever knew what it cost her to choose you. Although she was content to play auntie, I know she would have loved to watch Gloria grow up. To play an active part in her life. If only you hadn't come back, she could have married one of her many local suitors, stayed in Seattle, and watched her girl become a woman. Instead, you swept her away with you and she was doomed to watch from afar.

I don't believe Helen ever stopped loving you. Not during that long absence and first pregnancy, nor any time after. Does that satisfy your vanity? Give you faith in true love? She finally came to believe you really loved her. I have to give you credit for that.

I don't know whether it pained Helen to keep your child a secret from you. I don't know whether she ever cried for Gloria. I'm not sure you would have found anything suspicious about her great fondness for her niece.

There were worries, of course. I thanked God every day that Gloria looked nothing like you, while dreading that some resemblance would eventually show. But she looked too much like Helen and me. I shrugged off the resemblance as a happy coincidence and hinted that my "friend" was a distant cousin.

If Mama and Papa ever suspected the truth, they never mentioned it to me.

And so there you have it, Rans. The truth, finally. You do have an heir, an American heir. Not that it does you any good, all of your children and grandchildren being female. And Gloria being illegitimate. But if it's any comfort, your line lives on.

I do have one favor to ask. I've lived a long and full life and enjoyed myself immensely. What I haven't done is accumulate wealth. Whatever I got from Mama and Papa is long gone. I have nothing to leave the next generation.

I'm asking you to leave something to your grandchildren when you go. For Helen's sake. It's what she would have wanted. It doesn't have to be much. Some valuable bauble of Helen's, perhaps? Or enough cash to give them a sound start in life. You've always been smart. Even if you decide not to reveal your true identity to them, I'm sure you can find a way to leave them something without arousing suspicion.

A letter is old-fashioned. I suppose I could have called. But letters are our way, aren't they? A thing from the past. And they can be destroyed, burned in the fire, and no one will be the wiser.

Do what you will, Rans. Take this secret to your grave or go meet the newest member of your family line. In case you have any curiosity about her, I've enclosed a picture of your great-granddaughter, Haley. She's a little beauty if I do say so myself. Looks a lot like Helen did as a baby.

It's been a grand life, hasn't it?
Good luck, Rans, whatever you decide.
All my love,
Your devoted sister-in-law,
Clara

I took my time rereading the letter. By the time I finished, I had tears in my eyes. And a lump in my throat from seeing my name mentioned. I reread several key passages over and over.

There was no picture of me remaining in the envelope. I wondered what he'd done with it. Where could he have put it? Finding it in this monstrosity of a house would be next to impossible. Or had he tossed it? Torn it up?

I carefully folded the letter and put it back in the Bible with trembling hands.

My great-grandmothers, both of them, had loved me extraordinarily. Helen, enough to give my grandmother up so generations of us could have good lives and her family's good name could remain intact. Clara enough to love me as her own great-grandchild.

And Rans? What had he thought when he'd read the letter? Why hadn't he jumped on the first jet to America to see me? Why hadn't he introduced himself as who he really was? Why had he kept the secret all these years? Had it given him comfort to know we existed? Or caused him pain? How could he stand missing out on our lives? And yet he had called me here now.

Maybe I should have been furious with him. Maybe I was too forgiving. But I'd come to love the old Dead Duke, flaws, eccentricities, and all. Maybe it was in our blood to understand each other. Or maybe he'd simply done a superior job of laying out his case for me.

I understood. He was granting Clara's last request on a grand scale.

I shook my head. I still couldn't think of him as my great-grandfather. That was surreal. He was much too larger than life to be a mere great-grandpa to me. I was torn between regret that I never got to meet him and intimidation at the thought.

Whatever he was, he was making things up to us. And making sure his bloodline, the rightful line, continued in the ducal line. It was ingenious and cunning. Almost diabolically clever.

I realized with a start just how many years he'd been planning this. Had he been watching over us like a benign grandfather all along?

Thoughts rattled and bounced around my mind, seemingly random, and yet a pattern emerged. I remembered, vaguely, my parents needing money. I was young. The details were foggy from first memory. I just remembered the hushed conversations and worried looks on my parents' faces. Would they lose the baby?

Sid!

It was when they were trying to adopt Sid. They got the money from somewhere. Where? Where?

I squinted, deep in thought.

An unexpected windfall. Some distant relative had died and left them just what they needed!

"Damn."

My heart raced. My hands shook. I held the Bible tightly and shook my head, trying to remember. I was only four when we got Sid. All the memories from then were fuzzy first memories of life.

I took a deep breath. The Dead Duke. It had to have been. If he gave Mom and Dad the money, then he knew what was going on. Was there more to it than that? Had he gone as far as setting up the adoption?

I was both giddy and sick at the thought.

Was that why he knew how to find the cure for Sid? Because he'd arranged the adoption in the first place? And if he had, why had he picked a Chinese orphanage? A half-Chinese, half-Caucasian girl?

Oh my God. What if Sid was half British? What was the connection to Witham House and the Dead Duke? There had to be a connection.

I took a deep breath and reminded myself to breathe slow and steadily. I was onto something. I was getting closer to the thing Rans wanted me to find. To Sid's cure.

Just how far into my life did the Dead Duke's tendrils entwine? If he'd set up Sid's adoption, like I suspected, had he also planned this marriage from the beginning? Had he figuratively stood over my cradle like a fairy godfather, or a feudal king, and decided to arrange for me to marry his heir?

Had he watched me grow? Kept tabs to see if I was worthy to inherit? Looked for ways to bring Riggins and me together from the start?

I probably should have felt like a puppet in the Dead Duke's game of life. Instead I was filled with a sense of awe and destiny. I'd been deemed worthy to carry on the Feldhem line. I'd been given great wealth and responsibility.

I wouldn't let my great-grandfather down. The Dead Duke could count on me to take care of our dukedom. Not even Riggins could stop me.

I smiled to myself and realized I was grinning at the Bible. I had to keep this letter safe. I slid to my feet. And what better way to protect it than hiding it in plain sight? In the library. Out of order, of course. Sorry, Dead Duke!

I put my slippers on. And then, on a whim, I texted the photo of the letter to Riggins. He deserved to know who and what he was up against. He thought the Dead Duke was determined to get his way! He hadn't seen *anything* yet.

CHAPTER THREE

Riggins

I gave the woman two million dollars' worth of lingerie and she sent me a damn thank you text. And a picture of an old letter. To be technically correct, I'd left the valuable lingerie behind. So was it a gift? Or a statement about how much she'd lost by her deceit and betrayal?

I was still shaking with anger and hurt as I lay in bed and stared up at the canopy above me. Everything in this damn castle was ornate and antiquated. I longed for the sleek, modern lines of my home in Seattle. I didn't want to live in another century. I liked the twenty-first century just fine.

I wanted my old life back. The one where I expected people to let me down and women to sleep with me for my money. It was the betrayal that hurt the worst. Haley had seemed so honest.

Oh, shit, of course I knew who was behind the leak to the media. Rose. Who else? Haley would have told me about the baby, probably sooner rather than later. I didn't know Rose's exact motives, but revenge was a probable cause. She didn't understand that I wouldn't want her, even if given the opportunity. I could have chosen her, had I been inclined. Or so I'd thought at the time.

As nasty as it was, I couldn't get the niggling concern out of my mind that Haley had gotten pregnant on purpose. Yeah, I knew I was complicit. But...I shouldn't have had to wear a condom every damn time when she'd assured me she was on the pill. Was that all a ruse?

I read her text again.

Don't say it. Don't ever say that you don't want this baby. You'll regret it forever.

I swallowed hard, gulping back my guilt and thinking about my old man. Did I have any sympathy for him now? What if he hadn't wanted to be a father either? Was that an excuse worthy of not manning up to the task?

Was Haley right? Would I regret it? Anger was a nasty, blinding beast, and I was furious right now. There was more to her text.

You can say whatever else you want to me or about me. Yell and scream. Call me names. Even threaten to throw me out. But don't reject your child. Don't pass that legacy on.

And whatever else you're thinking or imagining, I didn't plan this pregnancy. I didn't trap you into anything. I'm as surprised as you are.

Surprised, was she? I was in shock.

But I'm already in love with this baby. Partly because it's yours. Yeah, you big douche. Get over yourself and I think you'll come to your senses.

I know. It's the shock. I've had longer to get used to the idea. Give it some time to sink in and you'll realize this is the best thing that ever happened to you, too. This isn't how I wanted you to find out, but it is what it is.

And as for you and me, read the letter. We're fated to be together.

Thanks for the bra and panties. Won't they be a scandalous addition to the duchess' jewels?

I smiled despite myself at her attempt at humor, picturing future duchesses parading around in their tiaras and diamond underwear. Very dignified. The other dukes may have had their extravagances, but diamond and jeweled lingerie? That was a new excess.

My amusement was short-lived. I scowled. Damn her. My heart pounded. I swallowed hard. I wanted her worse than anything. So desperately I was feverish for her. I wanted her to be guileless and telling the truth. I needed her to be the Haley I'd fallen in love with. Which raised the question—assuming Haley was telling the truth, how *did* our birth control fail?

I read Clara's letter for the third time.

Rans, you dead bastard, we've both been taken in by women. Two women who look eerily alike.

Haley

I called Sid, still trembling. I had to tell her about the baby before the news reached her. I'd always imagined telling her in some fun way. Curses on Rose for ruining things.

I glanced at the clock. It was the middle of the afternoon in Seattle. Sid would be out of class and hopefully someplace she could talk.

When she picked up on the second ring, I nearly collapsed with relief.

"So. Are you wearing that diamond-crusted bra Riggins is rumored to have bought before he jumped on a plane and raced to you?" she said.

At the sound of her voice, I almost cried. I missed her, obviously, but I hadn't realized just how much.

"What?" I was momentarily caught off guard by her flippancy.

"Oops! Obviously not, I guess." She laughed. "I hope I didn't spoil the surprise. If he bought it for a mistress, I'm going to kill him myself."

"Since when did his underwear-buying habits become public?" I bit my lip.

"Since he became a duke and a billionaire. It's all over the entertainment news." She laughed again. "So is it true? Are you wearing diamond underwear right now?"

"Not exactly. Though I can confirm I'm in possession of a jewel-encrusted lingerie set." I paused, hoping that the underwear was *all* that had been in the American press and that social media hadn't picked up the British story. Poor Riggins. It was hard to keep a surprise secret.

How much had someone been paid for the diamond underwear story? At least Rose wasn't the prime suspect this time. "Has anything *else* about us been in the news?"

"No." There was a suspicious frown in her voice. "Is there something I should know?"

"I'm pregnant," I blurted inelegantly. "Half of England already knows. Don't blame me. Rose sold the story."

Before Sid could either squeal with delight or chastise me, the whole story tumbled out. Everything. Clara's letter to the Dead Duke and all its contents. Riggins walking in. The bruised roses. The bra and panties in the box. I seemed unable to stop myself.

To Sid's credit, she didn't interrupt.

"Wow," she said when I finished. "That's all I've got. I'm thrilled for you. I'm going to be an auntie!" She laughed, genuinely psyched and happy sounding. "Way to go, sis!"

"Didn't you hear the part about Riggins being very angry with me? To the point of livid."

She laughed again. "What does *he* matter? It's all immaterial now. He can't divorce you, even if he wants to, without losing Flashionista and everything he's worked for. At least not until little baby heir is born.

"I can't tell you how proud I am! You finally listened to little sis, got knocked up, and now your future is secure." She was teasing. At least partially.

"Yeah, that's the problem." I sighed. "That's what Riggins thinks—that I trapped him into fatherhood."

"Well, he trapped you into marriage. So there's that."

"No, the Dead Duke trapped us both."

She ignored that fact. "Riggins will come around. Especially once he sees the adorable baby you're going to pop out. The two of you are such a gorgeous couple—how could your baby be anything short of adorable?"

I shook my head. She was trying to cheer me up. And it was working, to a degree. "I hope you're right. But it could be a *long* seven and a half months until the baby's born."

"Not so long. You have that diamond fantasy bra to keep you company. And if worse comes to worst, you can always hock it."

"What if Riggins goes AWOL on me?" My heart broke at the thought.

"Disappear from Flash and a dukedom? It's not likely, is it?"

"My baby sis, the eternal optimist!" I could almost hear her smile. "The thing is—I don't know how I got pregnant—"

"If you don't know that yet, Hale, I can't help you. Do I have to explain the birds and the bees to you? When you and Riggins get naked together and he puts his—"

"Shut up!" I smiled softly.

Sid! She really did cheer me up.

"I should have been clearer. I have no idea how my birth control failed. I was so faithful..."

And then it hit me—given his mastery of manipulating lives, would the Dead Duke leave something as important as his heir's conception to chance? Wasn't that the main point of this entire adventure? If he'd manipulated everything as I suspected, why wouldn't he have done everything he could to make sure I got pregnant? Especially if he'd known, as I was sure he had, that Riggins didn't want to father an heir.

"Hale? Are you still there?" Sid's voice brought me back to the present.

I filed my suspicions away and turned my thoughts to more pleasant topics, the real thing I was excited about in all this drama.

"Sid, hang on. I'm going to text you Clara's letter so you can read it for yourself later." I quickly did so. "You know what this all means?" I said in a rush of excitement. "I think the Dead Duke has been watching us and manipulating our lives for even longer than we imagined."

My voice rose with enthusiasm as I told her my latest theory. "Sid, I think my great-grandfather arranged your adoption. That your father is British and somehow connected to the Dead Duke, at least peripherally."

I detailed my theory. "He didn't do anything that wasn't intentional. I'm guessing he was helping someone out. If I'm right, someone at the castle or in the

village might know something about it. I think the
Dead Duke is leaving me breadcrumbs."

I could almost see Sid's ears perk up. I wished we'd
been FaceTiming.

"Wow. That's a great theory." She paused. "You're
thinking we're both somehow connected to Witham
House?" There was excitement in her voice at the
thought. She laughed again. "Maybe *I'm* the Dead
Duke's bastard child. And the one true heir."

"It's not impossible," I said, running with the gag.

But it was preposterous. If she'd been the Dead
Duke's child, I was pretty sure Rans would have arranged for *her* to marry Riggins, not me. A child
trumped a great-granddaughter any day.

I looked upward, thinking and doing a little math in
my head. "If that's true, we're related by blood! And
that would make you not my half-sister." I concentrat-
ed. "My grandma?"

We both laughed because it was so ludicrous. Or
was it? We spent a good half-hour trying to figure out
what our relationship would be if Rans had sired her.
Talking with my fun-loving sister, I almost forgot my
problems with Riggins.

"Should I start calling you Granny?" I said to Sid.

"Don't you dare! Let me at least turn twenty-one
and go on my bar run before you age me like that.
Grannies have to act semi-respectably and sedate, and
I'm not ready for that."

I sighed. "You *have* to come to England, Sid. I need
you here. Together we'll play sleuth and find your sib-
ling."

"I can't," she said sadly. "Not until the quarter's over at school. End of June, Hale. But we'll talk every night and bounce conspiracy theories off each other, evaluate suspects, and scheme. In the meantime, you have some investigative legwork to do."

"Yes," I agreed. "Where do I start?"

"Make a list of everyone who was at the estate the year I was born. Everyone who worked there, even as a contractor or deliveryman or newspaper boy.

"Talk to Mr. Thorne. He's been the Dead Duke's solicitor for years. It's possible he knows something that he doesn't know he knows. Go to the village. Chat up the longtime residents. Gain their confidence. Get them talking about old times. Listen with enthusiasm. Espouse your love of learning all of the village's past.

"Use your capacity as the duchess for good, sis! *My* good. Call on your subjects and get the scoop."

"Did anyone ever tell you you're brilliant?" I beamed with pride for her. Too bad she couldn't see it.

"I don't know about *that*. Someone definitely needs to inform my profs."

"Brilliant sis, font of all wisdom, I need one more piece of advice. In the meantime, how do I deal with Riggins?"

"You're asking me for advice on men?" She sounded amused and pleased.

"You have more experience than I do," I said, honestly.

"You have to ask?" Her tone was wry. "This is a no-brainer. You kill him with kindness. Adore him. Go on as if he wants this baby as much as you do. Make him fall in love with the baby. Get his paternal instincts to kick in. You act the part of happy duchess and get the staff and public opinion on your side. Make it impossible for him to stay mad."

"Easier said than done." I sighed.

"Catching a fly has never been easy."

Our conversation wound down. I yawned, suddenly tired. This pregnancy wore me out at the most inconvenient times. "It's late here. I should go." Not that I would be able to sleep peacefully.

"Before you do. Promise you'll text a picture of you wearing that diamond bra and tell me how it feels. I can't even imagine..."

Riggins

Breakfast was laid out for us in the dining room like we were royalty. And expecting a large crowd. Warming trays of fat English sausages, bins of stewed tomatoes, toast racks full of toast that cooled too quickly. The excess. The waste. As I filled a plate, I made a note to talk to the staff and ask that it be scaled down when it was just Haley and me. A bowl of cereal and a cup of coffee were all I needed. Speaking of coffee, where the hell was it?

I poured myself a cup of the family blend of tea that Haley seemed to prefer and made a note to ask for coffee to be put out on the sideboard with breakfast.

The assistant chef who made breakfast came in with another warming pan of something. Eggs, I thought.

I caught her attention. "Do we have any coffee?"

"Sorry, sir." She looked properly apologetic and just a bit harried. "I'll get you some. I didn't know you'd be returning until I got in this morning. And then with the preparations for this afternoon..." She set the buffet pan over the warming flame. "The duchess prefers tea."

Yes, during my short absence the duchess had made herself completely at home and taken over the estate rather thoroughly. Tea! Traitor. And this was the buffet that was set out for one person? I didn't give a damn that she was eating for two; this was still too much food.

I held my temper. "Thank you. I should have brought some back with me from Seattle." I had connections and friends at Seattle's premier coffee company.

"I prefer a nice, dark Kenyan roast. Order some fresh. Overnight it if you have to." I rattled off a list of the coffees I wanted. "Whole bean, not ground." I shuddered at the thought. Ground coffee lost its flavor and went stale too quickly. "And if you don't mind, set up the grinder and pour-over gear in the buffet here, along with a pot of hot water or one of the coffee machines I bought.

"I'll make my own coffee fresh. I prefer it that way." I smiled at her. "Sorry to be such a coffee snob. I can't help it. Being from Seattle, I was raised on the stuff." I paused. "I suppose the Italians are worse."

She grinned, mollified—I hoped, anyway—and went about her business before bustling out of the room.

I frowned. Last night had been hell. I was bleary-eyed, tired, needed coffee full of caffeine, not tepid tea, and only slightly calmer than I'd been last night.

Haley strolled in just then looking lovely and irritatingly fresh. My heart flipped over, treacherously joyous at the sight of her. The pregnancy had only begun to show, and was only noticeable if you looked closely enough and knew the intimate curves of her body the way I did. Her slender waist had grown thicker and her breasts lusher. There were hints of circles beneath her eyes that she'd carefully covered with concealer.

She smiled when she saw me, as if nothing ugly had happened between us last night.

What is her game? I scowled and turned away.

She caught my arm and kissed my cheek when she couldn't capture my mouth. "If it isn't my handsome duke! How did you sleep last night, darling?"

Darling? Now she was just baiting me.

When I answered with a glare, she looped her arm through mine and snagged a piece of dry toast off my plate. "Lovely of you to share. I need my nourishment. We have a big day ahead of us. Speaking of which, I hope your calendar is clear. We have a doctor appointment at eleven in the village. Dr. Turner has graciously squeezed us in on a moment's notice."

Her grin was lopsided and confident as she whispered, "The perks of being the duchess."

I stared at her in disbelief. "Dr. Turner?"

She smiled sweetly. "He delivers babies, duke. We need official confirmation before our official announcement in the gardens at four."

"What?"

She waved a hand breezily. "No need to worry. I've got it all handled. I contacted the press and made an appointment at the salon in the village to get my hair and nails done. There's an adorable little dress shop I'll need to pop into. You can come with!"

I regarded her with stony silence.

"Sorry, but this isn't the time to wear something from Flash. Not even by a British designer. Rumor has it that the shop owners in the village are feeling threatened by the thought of you taking Flash into the UK. Brick-and-mortar stores are already feeling the pinch from online buying. They're afraid of what a fashion flash sale site like Flash could do to their livings."

I was stunned and surprised by the thought. I should have been pleased by how savvy my duchess was.

"I think wearing something by a British designer purchased in a local shop is best for the occasion of announcing our first attempt at an heir. The gesture will go a long way to showing our support for the local economy, building goodwill, and allaying fears."

Gibson came in, interrupting before I could respond. He smiled when he saw us whispering to each other. I gathered he preferred domestic tranquility to the nasty, cold alternative. "Is everything satisfactory, sir? Madam?"

"Perfect, Gibson," Haley answered for us.

I said in her ear, "We need to talk. In private."

"Yes, of course." She was still smiling. "Your office? After we finish our breakfast."

She took another bite of toast. "I hope you have something dashing to wear to the announcement this afternoon. Something that photographs well. Ask Gibson for help." She winked at him. "I'm sure he'll have an opinion."

She squeezed my arm, grabbed the last slice of toast off my plate, and walked off, leaving me to stew like the horrible tomatoes the Brits insisted on serving for breakfast. Give me some American pancakes and Vermont maple syrup, damn it.

CHAPTER FOUR

Haley

Hearts can break in too many painful, shattering ways. As I waited for Riggins to show up for our after-breakfast confrontation, I was hanging on to the ragged edges of mine. It turns out that killing someone with kindness is not as easy as it sounds. Not when your own heart is under constant assault.

I wanted Riggins to want me. I needed him to need me *and* this baby. And to realize there were worse things in life than having a woman who happily carried his child.

I sat in the Dead Duke's chair—maybe I should start referring to him as Grandpa—sipping my morning Duke of Witham tea as I stared at the picture of him and Helen on the wall opposite the desk. My great-grandparents, I realized with a start. The reality was still sinking in, slowly.

By all rights, I should have grown up with this inheritance. I should have sat on the Dead Duke's knee as a child. Pulled his long gray beard. Did he have a long gray beard in old age? Played with his glasses. Ran wild through the maze and gardens. Explored the turrets and towers. Played scary hide and seek in the Ghost Tower. Been as familiar with this place as any grandchild should be. Have known my family legacy instead of being a stranger to it.

If only Helen had told Rans about Gloria. If only she hadn't let pride stop her. Or shame. Or love. That was what Clara claimed, that Helen hadn't wanted to marry Rans unless he loved her. And that she didn't want to trap him into marriage with a child. Well, that part was implied, anyway.

And here I was, holding Riggins to me with a child. Not by choice. But Helen hadn't really had *much* of a choice either. Still, which one of us was in the right in the end—me or her? Had she been right to consider her barren sister's happiness and her own over the legacy her child deserved?

Or was I in the right, fighting for my child to have its birthright and carry on a family tradition that I thought was worth saving? Was I right to fight for a man I loved using any method possible, underhanded if necessary, including a child I hadn't meant to conceive? Or had she been right to set her man free and absolve him of any obligation and any choice in the matter? Had he had the right to know about his own baby?

Speaking of that baby, some things made sense now. All those miscarriages Helen had? The result of the Rh factor problem between her and Rans. The first baby wasn't affected and was healthy, as Gloria was. It was after that, with subsequent pregnancies, that the mother's body attacked the growing fetus as if it was an infection or disease. Rans and Helen had been fortunate, indeed, to have one subsequent birth that went to full term and lived for almost a year. If I had to guess, that child had an undetected heart defect of some kind. That was the usual problem.

My own mom would have said you play the hand fate deals you. You play it not knowing what cards life holds. And you do your best with it. No second-guessing. No Monday morning quarterbacking. Full speed. Full throttle, making your way to your destiny.

I could almost hear her telling me this again. See her face soften with love as she encouraged me. Thinking of her had given me the courage to overcome my fear of the unknown British healthcare system and call the village obstetrician for an appointment.

There was no need for secrecy from the village now. Riggins would have to face this. And I would have to face a healthcare system I was unfamiliar with. And a press I wanted to shy away from. I'd have to live a public life until I was old enough and eccentric enough to be the old duchess.

"So, Helen, we're each doing our best," I said to the photo of my great-grandparents. It felt good to say it aloud.

Even though she continued in her duke's passionate embrace, I felt she approved. And so did he. I put my hand protectively on my abdomen, praying for a boy, as so many newly married duchesses had before me.

I started as the office door opened and Riggins strolled in. His face was set and hard. All business. Even etched with anger, he was so handsome he made my heart squeeze, shackled in the bonds of the love I felt for him.

I was sitting in the duke's chair, but I had no intention of giving up the power position and offering it to him. As far as I was concerned, this place was as much rightfully mine as his. If princesses could now ascend the throne, it was high time the female line should have rights to a dukedom. My great-grandfather, that ancient introverted hermit, had handed me this opportunity. I wasn't handing it back to anyone. Least of all a distant relation that didn't want what he'd been given.

Riggins didn't take a seat or say a word. He closed the door behind him and crossed the room to the window, staring out at the gardens and Capability Brown's capable landscape. "Cancel your appointment. I'm sending you back to the States to see a proper obstetrician."

Let the game of chicken begin.

I lifted my chin, in a show of defiance and confidence I didn't feel. If I kept this posture up, they'd have to start calling me the haughty duchess.

"I don't take orders from you or *anyone.*" I softened my tone. More flies with honey. "I'm not cancelling *our* appointment. And I'm staying here until I find Sid's cure.

"Dr. Turner in the village is very good, from what I hear. He's delivered over half the village in his twenty-five years practicing here."

Riggins crossed his arms. Even closed off to me and angry, he looked handsomely ducal standing there posed against the sunlight silhouetting him.

"I'm taking a cue from the prince and princess. We're going to be a duke and duchess of the people. And, as such, barring any unforeseen medical compli-cation, we're going to use the doctor everyone else on the estate and village does. Like regular people. Like the regular people we are."

"You're pushing too hard." He turned his gaze to me.

His eyes were in shadow. I couldn't read them.

I got out of my chair and went to him, taking him by his crossed arms and staring up into his eyes. "You aren't thinking straight, Riggins. When your anger clears, I hope you come to your senses. Maybe then you'll realize what a gift this is." I paused. "You've read Clara's letter?"

He nodded, still silently angry.

I refused to let the tension unnerve me. "Good. Then you understand my rights to this place. Legal or not, I'm the heir, too. My great-grandfather wanted this for me. You should be able to understand that, although I never cared about family history until now, I feel somewhat cheated out of my legacy."

He didn't answer, but his Adam's apple bobbed. I was getting to him.

"I won't cheat our baby out of its rightful place in life."

His eyes were still hard. I shook him gently by the arms. Not that he really moved, but I gave him the best shake I could.

"If you read that letter carefully, you must have realized something else—just how deep the Dead Duke's tendrils extend into our lives and just how long he's been manipulating things." I paused for effect. "My entire lifetime, Riggins. And most of yours—maybe all of it, for all we know."

When Riggins didn't respond, I continued. "It's clear he wanted me to be the duchess from my birth. For his own reasons, I suppose. I like to believe that, at least on some level, he had my best interests at heart, too.

"You're angry. You think I tricked you and got pregnant on purpose. That I broke my word. If that were true, I can understand why you'd be hurt. So maybe you can understand why I'm stinging from the way you jumped to a conclusion and obviously believe the worst in me.

"I didn't trick you, Riggins. This isn't my fault. I took my birth control pills religiously. From my point of view, one of two things happened. Either we're the 'unlucky' one percent who experienced birth control failure, even when using it properly. Or the Dead Duke has once again manipulated us from the grave."

Riggins' eyes flashed. His brow furrowed. He looked suddenly interested.

"Do you really think, knowing how closely he studied us, and how much he wanted an heir, that he would leave it up to us to conceive? Don't you think he knew that neither of us could really be tempted by the money? That we were each really blackmailed into this? And we'd try to fight for our freedom.

"I think he knew our natures and personalities almost as well as we do. Maybe better, in some ways. He certainly had the power of a distance, perspective, and objectivity. He would have known neither of us would just bend over and do what he commanded.

"He lured us here, Riggins, where he had more control. He knew we'd have to come eventually. And then, I'm not sure how he did it, but he tampered with our birth control."

I pulled my pill pack from my pocket and pressed it into Riggins' hand, relieved to be handing it over. Riggins was motivated and would know what to do with it. Had it been tampered with? I wanted the answer badly.

"Take these. Have them tested. See if they're genuine or if they've been replaced with placebos. I realize that even if they're placebos that doesn't prove my innocence. But think of this, Riggins—if I was so desperate to conceive, and such a conniver, I would have gone home to Seattle with you.

"I couldn't have known I was pregnant when you left. It was too soon. Why would I chance sending you off and losing your interest? I can't have sex with you across the pond, not the way I need to get pregnant, anyway. It would have been in my best interests to stay by your side until I was certain I'd accomplished my goal."

He finally spoke. "You really think the Dead Duke duped us?" His expression had softened and his stance relaxed.

I nodded. "If he's done even half of what I suspect him of, I think he's capable of *anything*. It makes me wonder what else he has up his sleeve for us."

I took a deep breath. "In the meantime, you and I have to keep up the public front. We have to look like we're complying with the Dead Duke's wishes and totally thrilled with our baby news. *Both* of us have to keep up the act. Or risk triggering the next mousetrap that my evil genius of a great-grandfather set up to ensure we don't escape."

I leaned into Riggins, got in his face, went up on my toes, and stood practically nose to nose with him. "Forget the terms he laid out. Rans isn't going to let us escape his will. Not without a fantastic fight and a lot of outwitting. We'll have to outplay him.

"We have no choice now. We played right into his hands, walked into his diabolical trap. I'm pregnant, Riggins. Whether we want to or not, we're going to have a child together.

"Let's have this baby *together* and see what happens. After we know what it is—boy or girl—then we can decide the fate of our marriage. Until then, everyone has to think we're still the happy newlyweds. If you don't want to endanger Flash, if you ever want your freedom, you'll have to play your part."

I took his face in my hands and pressed my lips to his. His lips were motionless, firmly set together, locking me out, rejecting me. It felt like kissing a warm statue. If he was going to be that way...

I ran my tongue lightly over his lips, tracing the firm outline of his mouth, pausing to circle the bow of his lips with my tongue. Working my way in, slowly, softly, coaxing him. *Open your mouth to me, duke.* Tantalizing, Teasing—

With one sudden, smooth move, he wrapped his arms around my waist. Startled, I gasped as he pressed me to him, kissing me back roughly, sticking his tongue deep into my mouth as if he wanted to possess me. I kissed him back eagerly, letting him hold me hostage with his kisses. He released me so suddenly I stumbled back.

He was breathing hard. "Damn it, Haley. I hope you're not playing me."

I'd tempted him. The anger protecting his heart was beginning to crack. It hadn't broken open. *Yet.* I'd just have to be patient.

I glanced at the clock. "We should be going. We have a doctor to see."

Riggins
The morning was sunny and calm, though cool. Highs were supposed to reach around fifty degrees. The view was pastoral, green, and peaceful. Idyllic. As long as you bundled up, the perfect setting and weather

for a stroll into the village. Not so very different from Seattle this time of year. But the setting was completely at odds with my black mood.

I was on a tightly wound string that was quickly fraying. My outlook dark. My mood grim. I was still stinging from the bite of betrayal. *Someone* had betrayed me. But damn, Haley had made me doubt my own doubt. She'd made a compelling case against the Dead Duke. Why did I have to fall for such a beautiful, intriguing, and apparently guilelessly logical woman?

On the surface, she appeared naively genuine. She was too easy to believe, and, because of that very quality, enabled my cynical self to doubt her. She could play me for a fool and I would gladly take the punishment she meted out. If there were only me to worry about. But now this baby. Shit. A baby.

It was possible my predecessor *had* manipulated us from birth like a fairy godfather in a storybook tale. Maybe there were landmines and traps ahead the likes of which we couldn't even begin to imagine. He'd had thirty-plus years to set them.

Maybe she *hadn't* betrayed me. Maybe *he* had. Maybe he'd trapped us both. *Again.* As frightening as the thought was, it gave me too much hope. I wanted Haley to be innocent of conniving to get pregnant. I wanted it so damn badly it hurt. I wanted her, pure and simple.

I was frustrated and furious at being manipulated and controlled. By anyone. Especially a dead guy.

There was no need to take the car. The village was right out our back door. Out the back of the castle, along the path across the green, through the fortress wall, across the ancient remnants of the moat, and there we were, in the village proper. It looked as quaint as the setting of a Jane Austen novel.

People were out enjoying the fair weather. Haley was full of smiles and friendly waves for everyone we met. The new duchess was quite obviously determined to win over the public. I found myself following her lead, nodding and smiling along with her, though I was forcing it. Giving her the benefit of all that shitty doubt, keeping a path open for us to come back together.

"Have you noticed, how very...white everyone in the village is," she whispered to me.

I nodded. I'd noticed, but I wondered what she was getting at. "Not as diverse as London or Seattle. Does it matter?"

"A half-Chinese person would stand out here, wouldn't he or she?"

I studied her without comment.

Her brow furrowed. "Someone has to know *something* about Sid's twin."

"You're making a lot of assumptions," I said evenly. I was furious as hell with her, but I understood where her desperation was coming from. I wanted a cure for Sid, too. "Even if the Dead Duke *was* helping someone out, there's no guarantee whoever it was came from either the estate or village."

She gave me a fierce look. "They were. They had to be. By the time Sid was born, the Dead Duke had become a hermit. There were very few people he cared about left. He'd buried three wives. He had no children, no brothers, no nephews, no near cousins. He'd outlived most of his friends and contemporaries.

"He would only have helped someone he was close to or fond of. Or felt responsible for."

"Or someone he'd bribed to carry out his dastardly plans for our lives." I laughed without humor.

She looked at me and momentarily frowned. Her face cleared, lit with a light bulb of a thought. "Excellent point. I'll add that to the list, along with this—or who would be important to the future of the estate. We know its survival was his ultimate goal.

"You could say, I suppose, that he was helping my mom, his granddaughter, by giving her another child, as she desperately wanted. But there's more to it than that. I'm certain there is.

"When I try to think as cunningly as he did, I have to imagine he was trying to find another way to bind me to the estate. At that point, no one suspected Sid would get this horrible anemia and he'd have that to hold over me.

"There's a connection between the Dead Duke and Sid. I can feel it. He placed her with us. For another reason. I think he wanted to bring her back to it at some point when he needed the leverage. At least, that was his plan when she was born. Then life threw him what he needed and his plan evolved with it.

"I've begged Sid to come. She wants to finish out the school year first."

Arguing with a hormonal pregnant woman, especially one as determined as Haley, was pointless. She was seeing Dead Duke conspiracies where there were none. I hoped.

"Here we are." She stopped suddenly in front of a quaint, old building.

Dr. Turner's office was in an ancient building that, at a guess, had been standing five hundred years. There was a date placard by the door. If I checked it, I bet I wouldn't be far off. In its checkered history, it could have been a variety of things. A pub. A stable. An inn. Or, hell, maybe it had been a midwife's house or a barbershop, back when barbers did any doctoring that was going to get done. Maybe it had a long, august history of midwifery.

It was built in the Tudor style, and one could almost imagine Shakespeare taking Mrs. Shakespeare there for her monthly prenatal check. Everything in the village was quaint and cobblestoned or covered in stucco or had decorative wooden beams. There was very little of the twenty-first century revealed in the historic facades.

The building was barely two blocks down the street from the fortress wall.

"Very convenient," I said, dryly, as I held the door to the building open for her.

"Don't be sardonic, duke. It doesn't suit you."

"I was just stating a fact."

The doctor's office was on the main floor, just down a hall and across from the village's only general practitioner's office. I paused with my hand on the door handle. My heart raced as if I was going to my own shotgun wedding. Shotgun daddy-hood—there was something new. "Ready?"

"As I'll ever be." She smiled sweetly at me, serene and eager.

I may have had the heart of a blackguard, but I felt guilty as hell for not sharing her joy.

"Smile," she said as I opened the door and let her walk past.

From waiting patient to receptionist, every head turned our way. There were only six chairs, but every one was filled with a woman at some point of pregnancy, and from their surprised expressions, their thoughts were pretty clear. *The tabloid stories are actually true? They must be. Why else would the duke and duchess visit the only ob in town?*

I smiled and nodded to them as Haley dragged me along to the receptionist counter to check in.

I'd reluctantly agreed with Haley's assessment of our situation and was playing the role of happy, hopefully expectant father. Not well, if my distorted reflection in the glass of a framed print on the wall was any indication. I looked more cynical and angry than exuberant.

Haley was all bubbles and effervescence. "We have an eleven o'clock with Dr. Turner?"

"Yes, Your Grace. We're expecting you." She glanced from Haley to me and signaled a nurse who'd been hovering in the background. Clearly, she was telling the truth. And we were getting the VIP treatment.

The nurse called us back and introduced herself as Dawn. Haley lost none of her excitement as she chatted up Dawn while she weighed and measured Haley.

Dawn showed her to the bathroom while I waited for the inevitable confirmation of impending fatherhood in an examination room with walls covered with posters of uteruses and babies in various stages of fetal development. Judging from the pictures, and counting back the weeks, our baby looked like an alien tadpole and was roughly the size of a sesame seed. But not as easy to spit out of my life.

Haley returned with Dawn, who gave her a minute to change into an examination gown. She returned a few minutes later to ask us a series of health-related questions and tap her answers into a computer. "Any family history of birth defects we should be aware of?"

Haley turned to me, crinkling the paper covering the examination table as she did. "None that I'm aware of on my side. Duke?"

I tried not to scowl. "I thought there were some babies born with heart problems on your side, duchess." I couldn't resist the jab.

"That was due to an Rh factor problem." Her voice was cool. "Since I'm O positive, that won't be a problem."

Dawn finished her questioning and left. Dr. Turner came in a few minutes later. The good doctor wasn't as old as I'd anticipated for having delivered half the town. He was tall and wiry, built like a long-distance runner, with thin gray hair and kind eyes. "You're definitely pregnant, Your Grace, but then, you knew that already."

Haley beamed.

I felt sick. Confirmation was hell on hope.

"Congratulations!" His voice was heartily cheery. "The village will celebrate. We'll finally have a chance to hear the bells ring announcing a new birth at the castle this fall. I've practiced in the village for twenty-plus years and never heard them." He smiled as he took a seat in the chair in front of the computer screen and read Haley's chart. "Everything looks good. Let's take a peek under the bonnet and see what we have."

I turned away while he examined my wife's private anatomy.

"Everything looks healthy," he said. "You can look now, sir." His voice had a laugh in it.

I turned around to face them as Haley sat up and adjusted herself.

"From what you've told me and what I can see, you appear to be five weeks along. I usually don't see patients until the eighth to tenth week. But you look to be right where you should be for this stage of early pregnancy.

"Our first order of business is to establish a due date, which by my calculations will be November ninth. We'll set up a series of appointments for you. Including one for twenty weeks where we can determine the sex of the baby with an ultrasound. We'll do the ultrasound either way, but you have the choice of finding out the sex—"

"Yes," I said, my voice hard and determined.

Haley and Dr. Turner turned to me. He wore a surprised expression. Maybe he hadn't expected such vehemence.

"A true duke. Eager for a son to pass the title to." The doctor's grin was tentative.

Haley gave me a warning look.

"Yes, of course," I said. "We're both eager to find out what we're having." If it were a boy, he'd be my way out of the marriage. Flash would be safe. And I'd be several hundred million richer. Was that what I wanted? Would I love a little girl just as much?

The truth was, although I'd never wanted children, if I ever considered having them at all, I was the odd guy who wanted girls.

The doctor picked up on the sudden surge of tension. His brow furrowed as he tried to figure out what had caused the sudden chill when he'd given us nothing but good news.

Haley lifted her chin. "Either gender will be welcome. But of course the duke is eager to pass his title on."

"Very good," the doctor said. "Will you be having the baby here, then? In the village? Or London? Or are you planning to return to the States to give birth?"

Haley looked to me for an answer.

"Sea—"

She cut me off. "We haven't discussed it. It's all still new to us. We just found out we were pregnant yesterday." Her smile was beautiful and happy. "We'll let you know as soon as we decide."

She hesitated. "I have an important question for you, doctor. I know it's usual to wait to announce a pregnancy until ten to twelve weeks along. To, you know, see if it sticks." She bit her lip, looking too damn vulnerable. "But the news, or rumors of it, anyway, is out already. So I thought...well...

"The duke and I have scheduled a press conference this afternoon to confirm the news and silence any rumors. We can cancel it, if you think that's best." She sounded suddenly young and uncertain.

The doctor patted her hand in a fatherly way. "I understand the concern. Normally, I would say wait. But in this case the pregnancy looks quite healthy. It's your private decision to make. But I don't see any danger signs."

She nodded and relaxed. "Thank you for putting my mind at ease. Whatever happens, I think the truth is always best." She flashed a challenging look at me. "If something does go wrong, it will be a comfort to have other people's support and not suffer in secrecy and silence."

She was talking to me again.

"It's an honor to be attending a duchess' pregnancy, in whatever capacity you allow. Attending to a high-profile aristocratic pregnancy will be a happy first in my career," Dr. Turner said. "I don't get too many firsts this late in life. Maybe some of your celebrity will rub off on me."

"I'm not sure you'll really want that celebrity once you get it," Haley said. "I wouldn't be surprised if a pack of reporters aren't already hanging about the lobby and trampling your lawn." Her laugh was tinkling and magical. She was so damned happy about this baby. "It's too bad the late duke never had children or grandchildren for you to deliver."

The doctor laughed. "Quite so. It was a disappointment to the entire village that there have been no heirs born here in the last hundred-odd years. It would have been a great honor to deliver one."

"I imagine you've delivered babies on the estate, though?" Haley arched a brow.

I knew what she was up to, but she was smooth.

Dr. Turner shook his head. "No. I can't rightly say I have. Old Gibson, of course, never married or had children that I know of.

"The gamekeeper, Bird, is the only one from the estate proper who's had children since I started my practice here. And him just the one son. I didn't deliver his boy. He was born out of the country. In China, I believe."

Haley tensed and her eyes lit up. I froze.

"Nice-looking, strapping lad," the doctor said. "Never favored his mother much. Looks like his father, but with all the best features. Nineteen or twenty by now, I believe. Away at university. I imagine you'll meet him soon enough when he comes home for break. He has aspirations to work at the castle for you like his father and carry on the family tradition.

"I believe his mother would have been proud of him, too, if she were still alive. Bird's been a widower now for over five years. It's a miracle one of the village widows hasn't snapped him up."

"Bird's wife was from around here?" Haley asked. She looked almost crestfallen, but was clearly trying to cover it.

"Yes, indeed. A local girl. She and Bird grew up together." Dr. Turner set his stethoscope on the counter.

"They're very lucky, then. It's lovely here." Haley sounded so genuine. "Very different from Seattle. Quite homogenous. Even the duke and I stick out as Americans, and we both have British heritage."

Dr. Turner laughed. "Well, I can't say as we've had many American dukes before." He grinned at me.

I thought that if I hadn't been the duke, he would have winked.

"But you're right," the doctor said. "We don't have the diversity of people or culture here that you'll find in London."

Haley was on fire as we left the doctor's office and headed to the post office to mail her birth control pills to the lab.

"We have to talk to Bird." Her voice was fierce with passion and her face set with determination.

"Haley—"

"No, don't." She took my arm. "It's too much coincidence that he was in China around the same time as Sid was born. He must know *something*. Either the duke sent him there to take care of things or—" She gasped. "He could be Sid's biological father—"

"Didn't you hear what Dr. Turner said? Bird's son is his and his wife's. At best, if Bird had an affair with a Chinese girl, the son of his we know about would be a half-sibling. Not the full one Thorne thinks exists."

"A half-sibling is better than nothing." The fierceness was on her face now. "My grandfather wasn't the monster you think he was. If you'd read his letters to Helen..."

She paused. "You must read his letters to Helen. He loved her and, by extension, me. I'm the last thing left of her. He knew I love Sid. He may not be above using her health to blackmail me. But I think he believed he was blackmailing me for my own good.

"He left a cure for Sid. I know he did. We just have to find him or her. I'm equally sure Rans hid it. But I'm his granddaughter. I have his wily mind. I'm only beginning to realize that."

CHAPTER FIVE

Haley

Riggins was quiet as we went to the post office and mailed my pills off to the lab he'd chosen for testing. Personally, I didn't think it was likely that they'd been tampered with. But I was desperate to find out how the Dead Duke had made sure I'd gotten pregnant. The first step was eliminating the obvious—substituting my pills with placebos. That would have been hard to do. But what would the results say to Riggins if the results came back that the pills were genuine? Would he think I was trying to throw him off course?

He had to believe that I wasn't duplicitous and complicit with the Dead Duke's plan for me to bear an heir.

Our relationship and future happiness depended on it. Even now, with the strain, suspicion, and doubt between us, I wanted Riggins more than life itself. I couldn't imagine life without him. Or with him only on the periphery as we shuttled a child between us. My plan hadn't changed—win his heart and find Sid's cure.

My mind whirled with possibilities. Why had I not known that Bird had gone to China around the time Sid was born? Why was he the one person on the estate that I hadn't met?

On the one hand, that was all completely logical. Other than delivering fresh game to the castle kitchen, there was little need for the gamekeeper to be at the castle. He had his own cottage on the edge of the estate and his job was in the field, not indoors.

The wildlife was Riggins' domain. By longstanding tradition, game management was the duke's purview, not the duchess'. My great-grandfather had known I wasn't interested in hunting or wildlife particularly, so why would I interfere with tradition?

No, the wily old man had counted on Riggins taking care of it, buying me time to get pregnant before I discovered Sid's cure. He wouldn't have wanted me to find the cure and get out of the deal before producing a child that bound.

But now I felt an urgency to talk to Bird. As soon as possible. First, though, I had to get through the rest of the day. The sun was shining and had warmth when you stood directly in it, though the air was still cool. The sunshine gave me courage. Riggins and I had unfinished business. Yes, he was stinging from thoughts of betrayal. I was hurting, too.

It had been foolish, maybe, to think he'd chosen me over Rose for myself. Before I knew about my true connection to Rans and Helen, I could even believe I was Riggins' choice. It had been a pleasant fantasy. But now that the results of the DNA test were clear and I knew about them, I was washed in doubt. It sounds stupid, really, but the sunny day gave me courage. What could possibly go wrong on a beautiful day like this? Besides everything?

The dress shop was a few blocks down and over from the post office. Everything was within comfortable walking distance of the castle and everything else. I loved the village. It had a relaxed feeling reminiscent of a simpler era, even though things were anything but uncomplicated for anyone. But it gave the illusion of it, anyway.

As we strolled to the shop, I nibbled on some crackers I'd brought with me in my oversize purse. We'd decided beforehand to have tea at the castle after we finished our errands. But I couldn't go long between meals without snacking on something.

I stopped suddenly, catching Riggins by surprise. "You knew I was Helen's grandchild as soon as the DNA results came back. That's what you meant by unusual results. I was too closely related to be a great-niece."

He gave me a startled look. "What?"

"You knew," I said again, watching him closely.

He shifted his weight from one foot to the other before finally nodding. "Yes."

"Did you check my DNA against the Dead Duke's?" I had to know. If he wasn't going to love me, I had to have a reason not to trust or love him.

"No." He held my gaze.

"But you must have suspected. Why else would the Dead Duke be so adamant that I had to marry you?" I couldn't understand his lack of curiosity.

"For the reason the will stated—that he wanted his and Helen's DNA to continue the line, meaning me and a descendant of Helen. I didn't question it. If he wanted to hand hundreds of millions over to a descendant of Helen and another man, it wasn't my business."

I looked him in the eye. "I don't believe that. You're not that incurious."

"You're calling me a liar?" His tone was surprisingly neutral, but his eyes were narrow, as if he was barely hanging on to his sense of control.

"I believe you didn't have my DNA tested against his. I don't believe your reason." I touched his arm, trying to be conciliatory without letting him completely off the hook.

His expression softened. "You're too damned sharp, duchess."

"You would have preferred a stupider woman?" I squeezed his arm.

He shook his head. "In this instance, maybe."

"So? Why didn't you check the DNA?" I wasn't giving up.

"Because I'm a coward." He covered my hand resting on his arm with his hand. "I didn't want to know the answer in case it obligated me to more than I was prepared to deal with. I talked to Thorne about the possibilities and asked if there was any way to give the estate to you in case you were the duke's great-granddaughter. Not that I had any intention of finding out for sure."

Riggins held my gaze. "Thorne explored it. But the will, and the poison pill, are airtight. I can't give the estate to you, even though you're from the direct line and the last heir of it.

"I'm sorry to shatter your illusions of him, Haley. The Dead Duke didn't just want his great-granddaughter to have the estate because of a sentimental notion of familial love. He wanted the estate intact with a duke from his line running it." He sounded genuinely sorry.

A lump formed in my throat. I nodded. "Don't be. I believe nothing less of him." I paused. "Are the DNA results you knew about why you chose me over Rose?"

"Partly."

"Oh." I looked up into his eyes, which were suddenly dancing with devilment. "Only partly? There's more to it?" My heart raced. I was hoping there was *much* more to it.

"I suppose I thought you would be more compliant."

I gave him a gentle shove.

"Clearly, I was wrong." He laughed softly. "I'm not the best judge of character."

"Obviously not." I smiled back at him, still looking for more.

Riggins took my arm. "Time to be doing the shops. We're keeping the shopkeeper waiting. Let's go buy you a new dress to wear to our big announcement."

It was a clever diversionary tactic, but eventually he would have to tell me his true feelings for me. "Your British is coming along quite nicely."

He grinned as we started walking. "I've been studying while I was gone. I had to do something to fill the lonely hours."

I looked up at him sharply, trying to see if he was still joking with me. He was looking straight ahead with an inscrutable expression, damn him.

The shopkeeper, Heidi, met us at the door and showed us to a private fitting room. Heidi was about Riggins' age, I guessed. And stylishly dressed. Her little shop was well laid out, gently perfumed, and elegantly stocked. Her mother, Linda, worked with her as her shop assistant and was on hand to help with my selection. This was an important event for them, too. And could mean a boatload of future business for them when word got out that they had outfitted the duchess for her press conference to announce her first pregnancy.

Riggins was shown an upholstered chair in the waiting area where I could parade in front of both him and a trifold mirror. I was shown to a fitting room where a rack of dresses in my size had been wheeled, waiting for me.

Linda and Heidi were both pleasant and friendly. It wasn't hard to get them chatting. In short order, I discovered they'd both been born and raised in the village. Heidi had gone away to London to fashion school and come home to set up shop. Linda was immensely proud of her daughter. Neither of them knew much about the late duke.

"Never met him," Linda said when I asked about him. "Kept himself to himself. The new duke is already much more friendly and available." She peeked in Riggins' direction, even though he was outside the closed door of the fitting room in the viewing area waiting for us.

Her eyes got a friendly sparkle. "And continuing the tradition of being very handsome, besides." She grinned at me. "We're proud of our dukes. The Dukes of Witham have a reputation for cutting fine figures. The late duke was reportedly quite handsome in his younger years, and not bad looking at the end, for a man in his hundreds." She winked.

Heidi and I chuckled with her.

"That seems to be the general consensus of the late duke," I said. "Why was he so reclusive? Does anybody know? Was he just shy? Or arrogant?" I slid into one of the dresses they'd pulled for me to try on.

"There might have been some arrogance. He was from another era," Linda said, "when the aristocracy had more power and respect. But I think he liked his solitude and didn't find much pleasure in other's company. We've been friends with the Bird family for years. They've never had but good to say about the late duke."

My ears perked up. But I also had to admit to a certain amount of deceit and spying. I had known of the connection between the families beforehand. Our chef, Alice, had mentioned it. Which was part of the reason I'd decided to get a new dress when I had a closetful that would do.

I'd made the arrangements as part of my general plan to check up on anyone who'd been with the castle for a long time, before I'd known Bird had gone to China. I was even more interested now.

"Bird, as we call your gamekeeper, has always spoken highly of the late duke. Said he was loyal to his employees and generous with them."

"That's good to hear," I said as Heidi zipped me into a dress. Back zippers were such a pain. I turned sideways and admired myself in the mirror, certain Riggins would have an opinion on the dress.

Heidi stood back. "Very pretty, madam."

I nodded, still studying myself. "We'll have to get the duke's opinion." I pursed my mouth, wondering if the dress was right for the occasion. "He has a good eye for fashion."

I turned to the other side to view myself from another angle. "Someone mentioned to me recently that Bird spent some time in China. Many years ago, I think?"

Linda nodded. "Yes, madam. Almost twenty, if I remember right. He spent a year, at least. The late duke sent him there to learn some Chinese techniques for keeping game and to look into get some rare Chinese birds for the estate. The late duke was rather fond of the rare and exotic."

"Bird's wife was alive then?" I asked. "She went with him?"

"She was." Linda nodded. "She joined him later, after he'd been there several months at least. She was a hard woman. Many thought the marriage wasn't particularly happy. It was certainly childless for many years. But she came back from China with a baby boy and seemingly happy about it. Though the marriage seemed strained for a long time after they came home. And there were never more children."

She smoothed the shoulders of my dress. "She was proud of her boy, though. Right up to the end. She passed away five years ago now. Cancer."

"Very sad." I faced the mirror head-on. It may have been subtle to everyone else, but I was sure I was already losing the definition of my waist. The dress I was trying on was belted and fitted at the waist. I wouldn't be able to wear it long at all. I bit my lip, not wanting to give away the news too soon, although the gossip was already all over the village. "I'm not sure about this one. Maybe something with an empire waist?"

Heidi smiled knowingly. "Certainly, madam. An empire waist would be smashing on you."

I turned my back to her to have her unzip the dress.

"You don't want to show this one to the duke before you take it off?" Heidi said.

"No. I can pass on this one on my own." I held in my breath as she unzipped me. "Bird has never remarried?"

Linda chimed in. "No, and there's many village women who'd be eager enough to catch him. I have a few friends myself who'd be up for the task of being Mrs. Bird. He comes from a respected family, has a good job and a nice cottage on your estate. For life, as the old duke stipulated." She winked at me. "There's more than one woman my age who wouldn't mind settling down on the estate."

I laughed. "Do you know—I haven't even been to the cottage. What do you think Mr. Bird would do if I paid him a surprise visit?" I wasn't joking. Not really. I had to talk to him.

"He'd jump right out of his skin. You'd give him the start of his life, I imagine." Heidi laughed. "I don't think he's used to entertaining, especially not duchesses."

"So why hasn't Bird remarried? Was the last Mrs. Bird the love of his life?" I slipped into another dress.

"I shouldn't say so," Linda said. "He was henpecked right to the end, which is sort of sad, given his name."

I nodded. My lips twitched. I liked these two women with their good humor.

Linda sighed. "He came back from China a changed man, though, he did. More serious. More melancholy than I remember him being when we were in school together years ago." Linda zipped me and tugged the dress until it hung perfectly. "You look lovely! You have to show the duke this one."

Riggins looked up from his phone when I walked in with Heidi beside me. I held my arms out and did a little spin in front of the mirrors for him.

Riggins raised an eyebrow. "Empire? A little obvious, isn't it?" He didn't seem concerned by Heidi and Linda's presence, or worried they'd catch his meaning. "You have a beautiful figure. Try something fitted at the waist and bodice. A full skirt will be fine if it has the right flare. But I'd prefer something that hugs the hips."

I turned to Heidi. "I told you he'd have an opinion."

We both burst out laughing. I ended up buying the first dress I'd tried on. And a hat. Because British ladies wore hats on important occasions. It was a perfectly dainty and totally outrageous hat, too. Riggins gave me no end of grief over it. And yet he'd joined in with Linda and Heidi when they insisted on it.

"But it will ruin my hair!" I protested lamely before caving to Heidi, Linda, and Riggins, and buying it. "I'm American. We don't wear hats unless it's winter, and then only knit beanies or something."

Riggins arched a brow and zinged one at me, clearly enjoying putting me in my place: "You're a British lady now, duchess. Don't forget it. British women love hats."

Yes, but give me a good old American baseball cap any day of the week. But only for casual days.

Riggins and I walked back to the castle companionably, but I longed for passion. I'd missed him so much.

I stopped at the castle wall in front of the entrance to the estate and took Riggins' hands. "Aren't you just a *little* bit happy about the baby? Neither of us planned it. I swear to you, I was as surprised about it as you. But since it's coming and there's nothing we can do about it..."

I wanted him to reassure me, even if he had to lie.

His gaze swept over me and rested at a point somewhere in the distance over my shoulder. "I've never been a kid person. They're not my thing."

"*They* don't have to be your thing, Riggins, for you to love your own child. Your own baby will be different."

He kept staring into the distance. "My old man bailed on me. The men that came and went in my mom's life were no example of fatherhood." His gaze met mine briefly. "I have no confidence I'll be a good dad. And if you can't do something right, why do it at all?"

He looked at the castle wall. "This is a hell of a legacy and responsibility to saddle a kid with. How will the baby grow up normal?"

"He or she will grow up with what's normal to them. And anyway, bad parenting isn't genetic."

The breeze ruffled his hair. I clenched my fist to keep from reaching up to brush it out of his eyes and caress his cheek. "Cheer up! With any luck, the Dead Duke has done something to ensure you'll be a great daddy and his heir will grow up completely competent and fit for this life."

"Now there's a comforting thought," Riggins said dryly.

"You're going to have to fake some enthusiasm this afternoon. People expect dukes to be absolutely thrilled about a possible heir. It's tradition."

When his eyes met mine again, the corners of his lips curled very slightly into the faintest of smiles.

"Fake it till we make it. You think that's the Dead Duke's plan for us?"

I gave in to my urge and ran my fingers lightly through his hair to comb it. The intimate touch brought up a memory of our romp in the poison garden, and with it all the promise between us. He remembered, too. I saw it in his face.

I dropped my hand. "Maybe. But I give him more credit for deviousness than that."

CHAPTER SIX

Haley

Lights flashed in our faces as Riggins and I stood arm in arm on the lawn outside the castle beneath a large white marquee, as the Brits called a tent used for social occasions.

I admit to having been confused when Gibson suggested renting a marquee. My study of British English hadn't included it. I wondered why we should rent a huge theater-type sign with flashing lights. Was this pregnancy really headliner material for a theater marquee? And wasn't a huge, gaudy sign just a little bit tacky?

Fortunately, he saw my confusion and described what he had in mind. And as it turned out, the tent was beautiful, especially decorated with flowers and baby-themed items. And warmed by outdoor propane heaters strategically placed.

Riggins wore a custom-made suit he'd picked up in London on one of his previous trips. And a tie in the colors of the family crest that cost several hundred dollars at least. I wore my new dress and hat with its spiraling protuberances of feathers and lace, as I gazed adoringly at the father-to-be, with no faking needed. I did adore him. In the way Helen had adored the Dead Duke even during the stage when she believed he only wanted her for her money. Life repeating itself. Right now, I knew Riggins needed me to protect his finances. But in a different way from the way Rans needed Helen. I hoped I got my happy ending, too. That Riggins would someday confess his undying, dedicated love. Standing so close to me, he should have worried that my hat would poke his eye out.

The setting was perfect. The castle featured nicely in the background of the photos and, although a few clouds scuttled by, the sky was mostly blue, and the lighting natural and flattering.

My smile should have felt frozen on my face, but it was genuinely planted there from joy. Being with Riggins, who was faking his joy at being an expectant father way too realistically, made me too happy for the smile to be anything but genuine. Honestly, I knew his joy wasn't real, but I was letting myself live in this fantasy world while it lasted.

I'd had tea and cakes set up for the press and the crowd of villagers we'd invited in for the big announcement. The tea table was covered with a white cloth and pastel baby-themed confetti in the shape of ducks and bunnies. The food was ready for the guests to dive into as soon as the press finished with us.

I was proud of Riggins.

He was charming and outgoing, completely at ease as he announced the due date. "November ninth."

That raised a few eyebrows. Almost every gaze in the crowd fell to my flat abdomen. I pressed a hand to it without thinking, self-conscious.

"It's early to be announcing a pregnancy, isn't it?" a reporter for one of the entertainment shows asked.

There was no baby bump to report or photograph yet. I was sure that was a disappointment.

Riggins laughed it off. "Traditionally speaking, yes. We'd have preferred to wait until the three-month mark. But since someone leaked the story..." His smile dazzled the crowed.

They laughed with him, not at us. He had them entranced. They were falling in love with their duke. The Dead Duke had neglected his social duties for far too long. People were hungry to vicariously live the aristocratic fantasy through us. Riggins picked up on that.

"About that," another member of the press said. "Rumor has it that the duchess' friend and former competitor for your heart, Lady Rose, leaked the story. Is that true?"

I froze and felt the nausea rise. I still wasn't sure whether I should feel fury at Rose or sympathy. She'd been desperate and I'd been unable to help. If the money from our story, which was only the truth, saved her family estate, shouldn't I be the bigger person and be happy for her? Even though it had been a breach of trust for her to share it, I would have helped her if I could have. If this was the form my help took, so be it.

Beside me, Riggins tensed, but his grin and charm didn't fail. "Frankly, I have no idea. It's not important. We're just happy to be expecting. This morning Dr. Turner gave us the good news the duchess is healthy and the pregnancy looks good. That's all that matters to me." He smiled at me in a way that took my breath away.

The crowd heaved a collective sigh. Wasn't that sweet? Wasn't he adorable the way he looked at the duchess and wanted that baby?

It would have been if it were true. Riggins, I realized with a start, was too good an actor to be trusted.

The questions flew. Where would we have the baby? Would we find out the sex before it was born? What plans did we have for the nursery? Who would be the designer? Would we get the same baby carriage the Duchess of Cambridge favored? Would the baby be a dual citizen?

Riggins gave non-answers, deflecting most of the questions with charisma and charm and the pat answer that it was still early days. We'd only just found out about the baby ourselves. Nothing was decided.

I watched the crowd as I let Riggins handle the press. Happy as I was, I was still in the throes of early pregnancy nausea and feeling peaked.

I recognized most of the people from the village, and, of course, the staff from the castle. I'd become on friendly terms with Mrs. Rees. We employed her cleaning service to do the castle housekeeping. She and her crew were in several days a week. There was the librarian and library staff from the village. Linda and Heidi from the dress shop. And over a hundred others.

In the last decades, the castle grounds had rarely been open to the public. People were naturally curious. There was always a discreet detail of security people around the castle. The Dead Duke had employed a security firm, and we did, too. It was only prudent. The dukes of old had their knights to protect and serve them. We had hired security guards, high-tech cameras, drone details, and a sophisticated alarm system. After all, the castle housed as many, or more, precious historical objects as most museums.

We'd hired an extra security detail to keep an eye on the crowd and keep wanderers out of the castle itself. The last thing we needed were interlopers in our inner sanctum. Because of the extra security, I wasn't too concerned as people wandered away from the main gathering. Other than the fact that I'd simply tossed that two-million-dollar set of lingerie in a drawer. *Oops.* Maybe I should lock that up with the duchess jewels. Then again, there were more valuable things in the castle. Like many of those paintings casually hanging on the walls.

A movement on the edges of the grounds near the maze caught my attention. A tall man lurked, cloaked in the shadows near the maze, his face hidden. There

was something vaguely familiar about him. The way he
was skulking around wasn't in his favor, either. Why
didn't he join the crowd? I made a note to have security
check him out.

The questioning finally ended. I was caught up in
my duty as hostess. I invited everyone to help them-
selves to tea and sweets, and mingled.

"Yes, lovely." "Thanks so much." "We're thrilled."
"Thanks for coming." "Yes, a little earl would be just
the thing." "At twenty weeks." "Yes, we plan on finding
out. The future of the dukedom hangs in the balance."
I repeated all these pleasantries again and again.

The entire time, I felt I was being watched. Riggins
was busy and involved in conversations of his own.
When I looked out at the maze, I caught a glimpse of
the man again.

I grabbed a security guard and pointed him toward
the maze. "I'm not sure. But if there's someone lurking,
I'd like to know their intentions."

"Yes, ma'am." The guard took off.

Riggins came up to me and whispered in my ear,
"Everything okay?"

I frowned. "I think so. I saw someone in the maze." I
smiled at him. "It's probably nothing. I've sent someone
out to check." On impulse, I kissed him. And lingered
long enough to express my interest. "You're doing
beautifully. I'm not going to be able to trust another
thing you ever say. You're such a fine actor. Or maybe
liar is the better word."

He actually smiled. "If business has taught me one
thing, it's how to put on a show."

The press conference party lasted no more than an hour and a half and was, by all accounts, a success. Our security team checked the maze and grounds, but could find no trace of the mysterious, lurking man. They scoured the grounds and checked the security feeds once more after the press and the guests left. There were no traces of him, or anyone.

As the guests left happy and excited, Alice made a point of pulling me aside and telling me how much goodwill we'd made with the village.

After the day I'd had I was exhausted. I went to my room to rest. And fell asleep as soon as I collapsed on the bed, without bothering to pull up a blanket. The most I'd done was kick off my shoes and take off my hat. And even that had taken supreme effort.

When I woke sometime later, my new dress was rumpled and it was already dark out. Someone had thrown a blanket over me and turned on the gas fireplace. In the old days, a maid would have had to come in to light the fire. This old castle could get cold in a hurry.

I glanced at the clock. It was nearly midnight. How had I slept so long? Pregnancy hormones had to be to blame. Growing a new life took more energy than I had.

Alice had texted me sometime before she went home for the day that she'd left a dinner tray in the fridge for Gibson to bring up when I was ready. The duke had taken his tray earlier and dined in his room. What was Riggins up to? Still trying to find a way to defeat my great-grandpa?

I sat up and rubbed my eyes. In the dark, even my comfortable room could feel a bit scary. Something about a castle that was hundreds of years old brought out the gothic in my imagination. Truthfully, when Riggins was gone, I'd holed up in my room for the night and didn't like to come out until morning.

The halls at night, even with electric lighting, could be intimidating and a little frightening. Footsteps echoed eerily on the tile floors. No plush, quiet wall-to-wall carpet like at home.

Riggins had been right about those paintings of our ancestors, too, staring down on us with their eyes appearing to follow us. And then there were the ghost stories, which weren't confined to the Ghost Tower. The castle had its own set of spooks. Even if many of them were reputed to be my ancestors, I wasn't keen to meet them.

Thankfully, my room had an en suite bathroom. Otherwise I'd be holding it all night. Risk venturing down the dark halls? Shudder. Dashing to the bathroom with my eyes closed, like I did at our normal-sized suburban home as a kid, was the other unappealing option. Not very dignified, or brave, for a duchess.

Even though my room had been modernized, there was no way to completely get the draft and dampness out of a castle. A creepy coldness could present itself at odd times. And you think a modern home creeks and groans. That's nothing compared to the noises a castle makes. There is a reason even perfectly normal castles get reputations for being haunted.

I stretched and got sleepily to my feet. The curtains weren't drawn. They loomed large, gaping holes to the outside world. If I turned on a light, I'd be even more in a fishbowl.

The night outside was cloudy and dark. I walked to the windowed alcove that jutted out from my room. On sunny days it was my favorite spot in the room. Its floor-to-ceiling windows on all three sides were beautiful. And obviously a relatively modern addition. If you can call two hundred years ago modern.

I paused before drawing the heavy drapes, and peered out. It had a view of the grounds stretching directly before it. There wasn't much to see on this cloudy night. Thankfully for my heart and imagination, no shadowy figures or big, sulfurous fire-breathing dogs moved in the maze. I had Sherlock Holmes to thank for that last fear.

If I stood at the window and looked off to the side, I had a clear view of the Ghost Tower. Generally, I didn't look that direction after dark. On purpose. The Ghost Tower still freaked me out. The stories I'd heard of it weren't pretty. A castle didn't stand for five hundred years without accumulating its share of gruesome history.

Today, for some reason, my gaze flicked past it. My heart stopped. There was a light, like from a candle, in one of the upper tower rooms. It flickered for an instant and disappeared.

My heart stood still. I felt myself pale.

"Riggins!" I ran for his room, which adjoined mine. "Riggins!"

His door was unlocked. I rushed in unannounced without even pausing to think he might be in bed already. If this had been the olden days, I might have worried about walking in on him with a chambermaid. Wasn't that what powerful old dukes did, screw innocent maids? Mine wouldn't. And wasn't. And he wasn't in bed, either.

He was sitting at his desk with his laptop open. He looked up when I charged in. "What's the matter?" He frowned in concern, taking in my rumpled dress and wild-eyed expression. "You look like you've seen a ghost."

"I think I have."

He pushed his chair back, stood, and came to me, pulling me into his arms, and laughed softly and reassuringly. "Score one for you! Not everyone is privileged with a visitation. Who did you see? Old Rans? Was he in your room looking for Helen? How did he look—old or young and in his prime? I'm hoping in his prime. When I come back to haunt this place, I sure as hell don't want to do it as an old man."

I rolled my eyes at the absurdity and snuggled into him, loving him for the way he put my fears at ease. "My great-grandfather isn't on our approved list of specters."

I shivered and used it as an excuse to burrow even deeper into his embrace and rest my head on his chest. There was no place I'd rather be than his arms. I belonged here, with him holding me. He made me feel safe and content, unafraid. Ready to take on the world. And maybe even the supernatural if necessary. I allowed myself to linger and breathe in the scent of him. But just for a moment. We had a ghost to chase.

I pulled back, grabbed his arm, and tugged him toward my room. "It was in the Ghost Tower. Come see. Maybe it will come back."

He reluctantly let himself be dragged to the window in my room. But the Ghost Tower was dark and serene.

Riggins arched a brow. "Was your ghost gruesome? Headless, maybe? Or dripping blood?"

"Don't try to scare me, duke." I pointed, feeling his heat as he stood behind me and rested his hand protectively on my shoulder. Maybe all that faking earlier was starting to work. "It was in that window. Just a flickering light. Are lights male or female?"

"I have no idea." He squinted, looking almost comically as if he was trying to use the powers of his mind to make it materialize again. Finally, he sighed. "You probably saw the security guard on his rounds."

I shook my head, adamant. "No. The Ghost Tower is always locked. The guards check the door on their rounds, but that's it. None of them go in there at night." I shuddered again. "It would be cruel to make them."

Riggins sighed. "I guess this means I'm going to have to do my husbandly duty and check out the things that go bump in the night." His tone was wry.

His turned toward the door.

I grabbed his arm. "No way! In the dark? At midnight? In the Ghost Tower? Didn't I just say not even the guards go in there? No one goes in there, duke. *No one.* And certainly not alone!"

He shrugged. "A ghost is the least of my worries. What's a ghost going to do to me? Walk through me? Take a swing at me and smash my jaw with his airy punch?"

"Scare you to death." I was serious.

He shook his head. "I don't scare easily. Someone has to check it out and make sure the tower is secure. We don't want any surprise attacks in the middle of the night."

"I'm coming with you!" I reached for a sweater that was hanging over the back of a chair nearby.

He grabbed me by both arms and looked me in the eyes. "If you think I'm letting my pregnant wife come with me to examine a strange sighting, you're crazy. If a ghost scares you to death, he'll be killing my potential heir, too. The Dead Duke and the public will never let me hear the end of that. The last thing I need is the Dead Duke tying me to this damn place and then haunting me the rest of my life. You're staying here." His voice was firm.

My heart was soft. Was he beginning to want the baby, even just a little? "Riggins—"

"Don't worry. I'll grab a security guy." He gave my arms a squeeze. "Don't go too-stupid-to-live horror movie heroine on me while I'm gone, either, and wander off after me unarmed. Stay put."

I bit my lip to keep from laughing. "If I wander off, I'll take a candlestick or grab a sword off the wall for protection."

He stared at me seriously. "No wandering off. Promise?"

I sighed. "Only if you report back. And take your phone with you. Text me if you run into trouble."

He rolled his eyes. "Sure. I'll text before I fall over dead of fear-induced heart failure." He grinned, released me, and strode for the door. "Lock your door after me."

I laughed. "Some precaution! Ghosts can walk through doors."

"Not the human kind." He pointed to the lock. "Lock it!"

I saluted and watched him leave, doing as he asked. What was he worried about? I knew what I was worried about—him.

CHAPTER SEVEN

Riggins

I wasn't a damn ghost hunter. I didn't get a kick out of hanging around in the dark with ghost-hunting equipment like my friend Lazer did. But I hauled ass out of Haley's room mostly to escape temptation and my own traitorous feelings. She was too damned vulnerable and enticing. Too much like a woman I could love for life, and yet I still didn't entirely trust her. I needed to get my head on straight.

And then there was the matter of the announcement this afternoon and the way we'd left the grounds open. I was more concerned about a vagrant taking up residence in the Ghost Tower than a ghost rattling around.

The castle had a security central command room in the main keep. I went straight there and talked to the security guard on duty. He routinely monitored the cameras through the night and was replaced in the morning by the dayshift guy. Our cameras covered every square inch of the castle, the immediate castle grounds, the surrounding buildings, including the Ghost Tower, and gardens.

The guard hadn't seen anyone or anything unusual. But the mention of a ghost piqued his interest. "I've been here over a year, sir, and never seen a ghost, or anything paranormal, in the Ghost Tower. Not even an orb." He looked disappointed. "Some of the other blokes who have been here longer have seen a thing or two that would curl your hair, though, sir. Things moving without explanation and such.

"The tower is locked up tight all the time. What with it having the dungeon in it and all, it's impenetrable once it's locked. I checked the doors when I came on shift. They were locked tight."

Which was vaguely reassuring.

We stored all security footage for twenty-four to forty-eight hours. I asked the guard to review the video. We ran back over the footage from the Ghost Tower for the last few hours. Nothing. Completely clean. No apparitions, otherworldly or human.

I could have written Haley's sighting off as a symptom of pregnancy or an overactive imagination brought on by exhaustion and the events of the day. But she'd never struck me as the flighty type.

"I'm going to the tower to check it out." I realized I had no weapon and nothing better than the light on my phone to light my path. And no idea where anyone kept a flashlight around here. I asked the guard for one.

He gave me a confused look. "You mean a torch, sir?"

"Yeah, a torch." If I remembered my British correctly.

He found me a flashlight and, over my protests, called the security guard on duty patrolling the grounds to meet me at the tower. "Procedure, sir."

I took the keys to the kingdom with me and met the other security guy at the tower. We stared at each other a minute before grinning.

"I feel like I'm in an episode of *Ghost Hunters*," I said.

He laughed, obviously relieved to see I felt the same way. "Don't give them any ideas, sir. They've been wanting to come out and set up their equipment in the tower overnight for years. The old duke wouldn't hear of it."

"The late duke didn't believe in ghosts?"

"No idea, sir, whether he did or didn't. Didn't like people he didn't know hanging about, that much was certain."

I considered the Dead Duke almost a demon in his own right. A ghost would have been a perfect companion for him. But he was a practical, logical, diabolical man from everything I could tell. Not the kind prone to believe in spooks.

"It seems like having a good verified ghost or two would be good for the castle's reputation," I said.

The security guy considered the idea. "Having a bona fide ghost might have drawn too much attention for the late duke's tastes. Too many people wanting a look around, if you know what I mean. All I know for sure is that the Ghost Tower has been off limits for as long as I've been here. No one allowed in at any time, and the key kept tightly clasped in his grace's cupboard."

I frowned.

The guard laughed again. "The old duke was one on his own, sir."

It took me a second to translate. *One of a kind.*

I nodded. "He certainly was."

The guard didn't know how right he was.

"I don't believe the duchess would like the idea of a verified ghost much, either. If she keeps seeing unexplained lights, we'll have to call them out just to put her mind at ease."

"You don't believe in ghosts, sir?" Given my reluctance to enter the tower, he seemed surprised. "If the duchess is afraid of them, we wouldn't want proof of them, would we? In her state, too, we wouldn't want her to have a fright."

His concern for Haley and the baby was touching. Haley had been busy winning absolutely everyone over.

"I've never seen sufficient proof ghosts exist." Even if they did, I wasn't worried about them. There were no records of poltergeist at the castle, and they were the most dangerous kind, weren't they? We were certainly no Amityville.

The first guard had been right. The tower was securely locked. Even with the key, it took some effort to get the door open. I made a note to get a locksmith to come put some graphite in it so it would work better.

Inside, we flipped on the lights. The tower had been wired for only basic electricity and the bare minimum of light fixtures and electrical outlets. The light bulbs were ancient yellow incandescent bulbs that seemed to struggle to penetrate much of the darkness.

The tower smelled damp and dusty. Like any hundred-plus-year-old building. It reminded me of the dank, musty smell prevalent in the basements of the Seattle underground. It was eerily quiet. Our footsteps echoed on the stone floors.

It was easy to imagine the smell of fear in here. A man could go crazy imprisoned in the dark of this place for months on end. His rush from sanity aided by all the ghost stories that I was sure were invented to help his slide into insanity along.

The guard and I checked the first floor. Including the dungeon, which was not lit. We didn't go down into the cells. We used our torches to light them as we did a quick scan of them. It was a miserable place with the chill of evil around it. I shivered and convinced myself the chill was the result of the cold night.

"Easy enough to see how a prisoner could go insane locked down there, sir."

I peered into the dungeon along with the guard. "Yes, it is."

After leaving the dungeon, we climbed the narrow spiral stairs and checked floor by floor. I wasn't sure if it was just me, but I detected the faintest scent of a familiar cologne from my childhood in the staircase. I went cold. "Do you smell something?"

The guard inhaled deeply. "No, sir." He looked apologetic. "But my allergies have been acting up lately."

I nodded, unsettled. My mom had always liked the scent of that cologne.

The guard was no help. Maybe I had imagined it. But it felt like someone had been here very recently. It was hard to tell in the dim light. I made a note to ask Gibson if anyone had been in the tower in the last few days. I was of the same opinion as the guard in the control room. Without a key, this place would be almost impossible to break in to, especially without being noticed or caught on camera.

After declaring it safe and empty, we locked it back up. The guard went back on patrol. I returned to the castle to report to Haley. But what was I going to tell her? That she'd imagined something? Or had actually seen a ghost?

I knew her door would be locked. But her room adjoined mine. I belatedly realized I hadn't locked my door in all the excitement. There was brilliance for you. Some protector of the realm I made. I went to her room through mine.

She wasn't expecting me. I found her standing in front of the mirror with her back to me, her lavender-tipped silvery hair softly spilling over her shoulders. She wore stiletto heels that gave her a good four inches of height. From the back, she looked naked. Except for the telltale jeweled strap of a pair of quarter-million-dollar thong panties that sparkled with diamonds, rubies, emeralds, and sapphires of every shade. The best part of all was her shapely butt, round and firm and pale, the most perfect jewel of all.

Her eyes went round, reflected in the mirror when she saw me. "I was just trying them on. Did you catch a ghost?"

I shook my head, bewitched by the sight of her. If I'd known a woman could look so beautiful in jeweled lingerie, I would have bought her some for our wedding night. "Nothing. The tower was quiet and empty. The security cameras didn't register any activity, either. Human or paranormal."

"Don't you need special cameras like Lazer had at Wareswood to catch ghosts in action?" As she turned around, the firelight caught the facets of the jewels on her bra.

She sparkled like a damn fairy from a dream. She was beautiful and almost more ethereal looking than any ghost I could imagine. The bra, which would have fit her original measurements perfectly, was now slightly tight and shoved her dazzling, jeweled breasts up enticingly.

It was hard to keep my eyes off that bra and those breasts.

She smiled at me. "What's the matter? Never seen a woman in jeweled underwear before?"

"On a runway. Not up close and personal." And not mine.

Damn, where had that thought come from? How much mine was Haley?

Haley

Of course he'd seen women in jeweled underwear before. And not simply in the pages of a magazine. He was Riggins Feldhem, billionaire Duke of Witham. Not some ordinary guy. Before me, he had supermodels falling all over him. Probably still would if not for me. But the flirting was too good and too much fun to stop. And I wouldn't be one-upped. Not with this fabulous jeweled lingerie fueling my confidence, my pregnancy hormones crying for sex, and my heart calling for Riggins.

"How about a pregnant woman in jeweled underwear?" I leaned back against the dresser and crossed my legs against the building ache, bracing myself with my arms. Pregnancy may have made me tired and nauseated. But it also gave me a desperate need for sex, and the only man I wanted was in front of me now.

"Not that I know of." His voice was deep and hoarse with desire.

"There's a first time for everything." I couldn't keep my own want out of my voice.

"I guess there is." He was still staring as he took a step toward me.

I held my ground, smiling as he walked toward me, daring him to keep advancing. And he did. Until he was standing inches from me, toe to toe. Eye to eye. Our lips a hairsbreadth apart. So close I could feel his heat and excitement. Smell his cologne. Feel his breath mingle with mine.

His eyes were dark and dilated. As much as I told myself to breathe, my breaths were shallow. My heartbeat pulsed in my ears. I'd never been this excited. He was coming back to me.

As I held his gaze, he slid his fingers between my breasts, which spilled over the jewel-trimmed edges of the bra. The bra was totally impractical on so many levels. Including the swirled jeweled embellishments that spread like small wings from the tops of each cup.

He grinned wickedly as he casually slid a finger between my breast and the weight of the jeweled bra. "This is some fine craftsmanship."

If I'd been bolder, or thought faster, I would have asked him if he meant the bra. Or me. But I was too addled by his nearness to think clearly. As in awe of him as the first time I'd seen him. Nearly as tongue-tied as the first time he'd come to the bakery. But more desperate now than even then. I felt our relationship hanging on our next moves. If he advanced, if he still wanted me, I had a chance at getting him back and keeping him.

For my part, I had to offer at least some resistance. I couldn't be too eager. He had to pay some kind of penance for doubting me. Not because I needed it. But he expected it. I wanted him to respect me, for now and ever.

Before I could respond, he bent his head and kissed the tops of my breasts, cupping them and lifting them to his lips. At first he kissed them slowly so I felt the full heat of his lips. "Very fine workmanship."

He squeezed them more tightly through their jeweled encasement and pressed up against me more firmly, nudging my closed legs open with his knee. Coaxing me to open up to him. Wedging himself in.

If he realized how open my heart was to him, he'd have complete power over me. I was his, through and through. *Forever.*

With pregnancy, my breasts had become firm, heavy, large, sore. And extremely sensitive in a powerful, sexual way that hadn't been tested yet by his touch. Rubbing against my clothes could get them to bud up and fill me with longing.

When he pulled one breast free from its jeweled armor, I sighed, filled with a powerful surge of desire. I went wet for him almost instantly.

I took his head gently in my hands and guided his mouth to my freed nipple, which was dark and erect and ready for him. At the first circle of his tongue over my nipple, I gasped and spread my legs, pulling his crotch into mine and rubbing against him wantonly. He took my nipple in his mouth and grazed it lightly with his teeth. Circled it with his tongue. I fought the rising tide within me. If I had ever doubted a woman could climax simply from having her breasts stimulated, I banished it now.

I was as hungry and eager as a sex-starved young man, trying to fight off a premature climax in just the same way. I wanted to wait for Riggins and feel him inside me. I needed the intimacy of a union. I need a reunion with him.

He freed my second breast. Rolled the nipple gently between his fingers, teasing it, murmuring praises and wonder.

I arched my back, thrusting my breasts out to him, playing with his hair, moaning softly as he brought me to the edge of orgasm as he sucked my breast.

"Riggins," I whispered, reaching for the hem of his shirt. "Take your shirt off. I want to feel your skin against mine."

He leaned back just enough to pull it off over his head and toss it away.

We stared at each other.

"What are you waiting for?" I studied him, tracing every line of his handsome face. I loved him too much. I wanted him too badly. "Just do it before I come without you."

"You're not ready," he whispered back. "You *can't* be ready yet."

I guided his hand beneath my thong. "Can't I?"

"Damn, you're wet and—"

"As erect as you are?" I reached for his fly, unzipped his pants, and pulled his erection out. He was ready for me, too.

And neither of us were going to hang on too much longer.

He gasped as I stroked him hard and positioned his tip around my thong panty at my opening.

"I've never made love to a woman wearing jeweled lingerie," he whispered as he paused and gazed into my eyes. "And certainly not to a pregnant woman in a fantasy bra and panties."

I cupped his face. "By a happy coincidence, I've never made love wearing a diamond bra and thong. Take me all the way, duke."

He grabbed my hips, digging his fingers in to hold me in place, and thrust inside me. I wrapped my legs around him and rocked with him.

We were wild and incautious, caught up in the act and oblivious to our surroundings. As we rocked into each other, the dresser banged against the wall with the beat of our lovemaking.

"Miss me?" He grazed my ear with his teeth.

"Terribly." I pressed against him, holding him to me as the jewels of my lingerie dug into his naked chest.

"How much?" He ran his tongue around the inside of my ear until I shivered.

"Horribly. Desperately." I dug my heels into him. "Stop talking and finish the job." I covered his mouth with a kiss.

He pounded into me again with such force I was afraid the mirror attached to the dresser would shatter as it thumped the wall. I released him from the kiss and closed my eyes. I would have cared more about the mirror and the safety of the antique dresser if I hadn't been senseless with need and filled with only him.

Another thrust and my scream filled the room. An orgasm rocked through me to my soul. There was only one man for me. I knew with certainty I'd never feel this heat with anyone else.

I trembled with the force of him, listening to his echoing grunt of completion. I came with enough power to force a surprised scream of pleasure from my lips.

I honestly didn't know how he could still be standing. I was limp and weak, held up by the dresser and him.

Legs wrapped around him, I leaned my forehead against his, eyes closed, and traced his sweaty chest gently with tips of my fingers, enjoying the feel of him.

Finally, I opened my eyes and kissed his shoulder. He had the indentation of hundreds of jewels on his chest.

"I've branded you with my underwear!" I traced one of the indentations and gave him a wry, apologetic grin.

He glanced at his chest and grinned back. "It's only temporary. And my own fault for holding you so close and buying you that lingerie in the first place. That was..." He took a deep breath. "The most awesome sex I've ever had."

I smiled and pressed my forehead to his again, feeling almost shy. "Me too. But then, I don't have a long yardstick to measure it by."

He laughed and kissed me lightly on the nose. "I do."

"I don't know whether that's reassuring or not."

"Let's put it this way. I was so lost in the moment, I didn't feel your jewels digging into me. Or if I did, I enjoyed it." He swept me into his arms, holding me tight against his chest, and carried me to the bed.

Which was a good thing, because I really didn't think I could walk.

He perched on one elbow, looking down at me. "You're so damn beautiful, duchess."

My heart raced as I waited for him to say the words I'd been longing to hear. But they didn't come.

Why did he have to be the man of my dreams—handsome, smart, funny? I almost said *I love you* to him right then. It was on the tip of my tongue. I held back. The time wasn't right.

CHAPTER EIGHT

Haley

Maybe sex can't heal everything, but our reunion on the Edwardian dresser at least thawed the chill between us, if not the distrust. No more separate bedrooms. At least not this night. We slept tangled in each other's arms.

I got up early, leaving Riggins sleeping soundly in my bed while I showered and dressed. I loved the look of him soft and relaxed in sleep with his hair tousled and his long limbs sprawled. I was half hoping I'd find him still sleeping. But he was awake and reading his tablet in bed when I stepped out of the bathroom.

He looked up and smiled at me. My fantasy bra and panties sat on my pillow next to him like crown jewels on a display pillow.

"Have you seen this?" He turned his tablet toward me. "All the pictures we posed for, and this is the one they chose to lead the story with." He sounded more amused than anything.

But my breath caught at the sight of the clandestine shot of me kissing Riggins on impulse at the reception and the caption that read, *A duke very much in love with his pregnant duchess.*

Throughout my life there had been pictures so beautiful or true or intriguing that I wanted to step into them and bring them to life. Photos that filled me with fantasy or longing for something that would probably never be. Pictures of hot guys I'd never date. Love so strong I was sure I'd never feel it. Families so perfect, how could they ever exist?

Improbably romantic embraces. Tropical locales where no one could feel a care. Photos of my parents like I'd never seen them—young, healthy, happy, and in love. Looking at them brought up a welling longing in me that was hard to put into words.

This simple photo was the worst of them all. I immediately understood the reporter's misperception. In that picture, Riggins loved me. It was clear from our pose, his posture, and the expression on his face. That picture was exactly the way I wanted my life to be, with that caption. I wanted my duke to love me.

But nothing in that picture was real. It was only faked.

I laughed, nervous I'd give myself away. "Leave it to the press to create a fairytale." I glanced away from it and pointed to the lingerie on my pillow. "Will you put that in the safe for me today?"

His face clouded over briefly. He nodded. "First thing."

I smiled a little too brightly. "Good. Thank you. I have a busy day planned. How about you?"

"Same." He raised an eyebrow. "What's on your agenda?"

"I have to see a man about a possible illegitimate daughter."

Riggins' expression froze. "Haley. *Don't.* Leave Bird out of this."

"How can I? He must know *something*. He was in China when Sid was born. That can't be coincidence." I smiled at Riggins and sat on the edge of the bed next to him.

He shook his head. "And he's a white guy, don't forget that." He shook his head. "So he must be Sid's bio dad. Is that the logic?"

"I'm not going to accuse him of anything. I'm just going to pop round his cottage and see if he's happy with it. Maybe suggest it could use some updating. A little remodeling or refresh might be in order—"

Riggins covered my hand on the bed with his. "He's a private guy. You'll only embarrass him."

I frowned. "What would you have me do, then?" I felt my anger and frustration rising. My moods were mercurial, scuttling over me like wisps of clouds in the

sky. I was easily upset. "With Sid's health in the balance?"

"Let me help you. Like I promised. Let me hire a
private eye to look into what Bird was doing in China
and see if there's any connection. I know someone
who's discreet. Thorne might be able to add a few clues
that will help us. Let's look into things further before
you start throwing accusations of fatherhood around."
He squeezed my hand.

Why hadn't I thought of that? My heart swelled
with affection for him. There went another of my rapidly changing moods. This one was sappily happy that
he remembered his word. And that we were on the
same team for this one.

"That would be...sweet of you." I smiled at him,
wanting him to take me in his arms. "But I need to
meet him, anyway. It's my duty as duchess." I leaned
toward him. "You wouldn't want me to be remiss in my
duties, would you?"

He smiled back. "Absolutely not. Just behave yourself."

"Meaning?"

"You know what the hell I mean."

He got up to take his shower, leaving me to read the
article about our announcement of our pregnancy and
stare at that picture. Yes, in that picture he *definitely*
loved me. If only I could believe that the camera really
didn't lie. Because if it didn't, he was hiding his feelings
from me. And maybe from himself. And there was hope
for us yet.

I took a quick breakfast in the dining room, where the buffet had been pared down at Riggins' request. Actually, I agreed with him. These days I preferred toast for breakfast. Toast and Duke of Witham tea. It was one thing that always appealed to me. Though recently I'd been taking it without sugar.

I left instructions with Mrs. Rees and her crew on which cleaning tasks were my top priority. And told Gibson my plans for the day. "I'll be out running errands this morning. This afternoon I'll be stopping by Bird's cottage for a brief visit and inspection. I've asked him to meet with me there. I'll take my tea around four."

I had an important errand to run. I knew perfectly well how to drive, but not on the wrong side of the road. And not in one of the expensive cars that belonged to the castle. The thought of driving one made me nervous. I ordered a car service to pick me up on the road in front of the castle. I didn't want Riggins to know what I was up to, and the walk would do me good.

On the way to meet the car, I stopped by the Ghost Tower. It was tall, gray, and foreboding. And locked tight. Riggins had said he and the security guard had locked it last night. He appeared to be right.

It looked imposing and impenetrable. I *had* seen a light there. I hadn't imagined it. And ghosts didn't typically use lights, did they? Or shine so brightly they glowed like a candle?

The building gave me the creeps. I hurried on and met my car just as it pulled up. "Glenrose Abbey," I told the driver.

Riggins

I was sleeping with my wife. And damn it, against my better judgment, I wanted to do it again and again. I got that idiotic grin on my face every time I thought about her.

Before our lives together could continue, I had to put my suspicions, all of them, to rest. I called Thorne and arranged a meeting with him in London. Then I called the security firm and security expert I kept on retainer and laid my concerns out to them. I also arranged a meeting with a private investigator in the London office of a well-respected international firm.

Finally, I called up an old friend and asked a favor. I needed a recommendation for a social media expert to manage Haley's social media presence, appearances, and meetings with the press. No more leaving her to the foraging dogs of publicity. She needed someone savvy to handle things for her. If another story like the leaked pregnancy one popped up, we needed to be on top of it.

Phone calls finished, I went to the Ghost Tower. It was less frightening in the daylight. And still locked tight. I walked around it, playing detective and looking for footprints and evidence. There had been too many people wandering the grounds. The area was covered with footprints in all shapes and sizes. And the cleanup crew had done a fucking fantastic job of cleaning up. There wasn't a cigarette butt or gum wrapper in sight.

I cursed beneath my breath. If what I suspected was true, I was dealing with someone highly intelligent and skilled at not being seen.

I let myself into the tower and flipped on the light. It was gloomy even in broad daylight. The floors, which had been covered with a fine layer of dust until recently, were marred with the footprints from last night of both myself and the guard. As closely as I studied them, I couldn't find any trace of a third pair of footprints. The dust didn't allow for leaving distinct enough markings.

The best I could say was that if a third person had been in the tower last night, he was about the same shoe size as either the guard or me. There were no other signs that anyone had visited. Short of having a forensic team fingerprint the whole place, an exercise in futility, I was pretty sure, there was nothing more I could do. Maybe what Haley had seen was simply a trick of the light. But what light? How much light was there at midnight?

Haley had to have been mistaken. I hoped like hell she was.

Haley

Glenrose Abbey, the Earl of Colchester's estate, was grand on the outside. But not nearly on the scale of Witham House. The difference in our ranks and financial status was blatantly clear. As it had been for hundreds of years, my family still outranked and outshone Rose's. Even the grounds, though beautifully manicured, were a miniature version of ours. It was clear that family property had been sold off to keep the estate going.

Glenrose Abbey was open for tourists April through September, Tuesday through Saturday. There was a posted sign at the entrance to the drive. In a few short weeks, paid visitors would be crawling all over the grounds. But now the estate was as quiet as the private residence it used to be all year long.

My car pulled to the front. The driver gave me a hand out. I asked him to wait for me. Unannounced visits could be such nasty surprises. I wasn't a fan of them, personally. I preferred to be neither the recipient nor the giver of them. I nearly lost my nerve. Imagining Sid laughing and encouraging me to master my inner bitch was the only thing that kept me going.

I lifted my chin. I was a duchess. I could do this. For Sid. Riggins. And my baby.

A teenage girl of about sixteen answered the bell. She bore a passing resemblance to Rose. Something through the eyes. She clearly knew who I was. She paled when she saw me.

I smiled and extended my hand. "Haley, Duchess of Witham."

"Yes, duchess. I know who you are." She looked nervously amused at my arrival. Like a spectator at a game. Eager to see a contest. Yet not convinced her team would win.

"You must be one of Rose's sisters. Is Rose around? Her tweets would seem to indicate she is." And was still lounging in bed. I arched a brow. "I'll wait for her in the sitting room. If you'd be so good as to announce me."

"This way." The girl motioned for me to follow her without denying anything. "The front rooms of the abbey are for the tourists. And filled with workers getting them ready for our season opening coming up. The family quarters are in back."

The family quarters were considerably shabbier than the front rooms of the abbey. The earl's dwindling fortunes were pretty obvious even at a mere glance. All the pomp and splendor he had left to his name was on display for the tourist season. It was also obvious he'd had to sell much of the family treasure, including valuable antique furniture. Even the rooms for show were more sparsely furnished than our rooms at the castle.

The furniture in the private quarters was from this century and not particularly expensive. Most of it was the cheap kind you bought in a box and assembled yourself. There were no pricey objects of art. And the walls were barren of anything but prints. All the family portraits were on display in the showy rooms of the castle open to the public. The room was tastefully enough done, but no more elegant than a flat any normal person would have.

I took a seat as the girl ran off, calling for Rose. Her voice was filled with the singsong excitement of *there's trouble coming for big sis.* She seemed delighted by the prospect.

I was half afraid Rose would refuse to see me. And prepared to get my way by any means necessary. Including a public Twitter war where I called her out to come downstairs and face me, lady to duchess. Was that a fair fight? I thought so. My money, righteous anger, and superior social position pitted against her celebrity and social media savvy. The air needed clearing, one way or another.

She kept me waiting a good fifteen minutes, probably on purpose. Just as I was composing a text warning her to show herself or else, she strolled into the sitting room looking less put together than normal. Her fifteen-minute toiletry hadn't been enough to give her her usual high-fashion glow and glamour.

I took a certain vindictive pleasure in being the more fashionable, elegant person. For once.

It would have been usual for us to greet each other with stiff hugs. Instead we stared at each other in silence.

"Well, don't you look lovely for so early in the morning," she said with a tinge of mocking humor in her voice. If she was afraid of me, she didn't show it.

It was enough to know she realized our role reversal. I had meant to wield the element of surprise to my favor. Good to know I was succeeding. "Thank you, Rose."

"What brings you here?" She stifled a yawn.

I could have been insulted. I would have if I'd believed she was actually bored, not simply needing her morning coffee. Or something. Maybe she took some kind of caffeinated tea to wake her up in the morning.

"You weren't at our pregnancy announcement party yesterday. I'm checking in to make sure you're feeling all right. We missed you."

She was clearly stunned by the complete audacity and absurdity of my statement. Missed her? Right. I was calling her out, and she knew it.

But Rose wasn't one to be taken off guard long. "And I was even sorrier to miss it. But it was unavoidable. I had to go to London. A prior appointment. Lovely photo circulating around the web, though. The two of you look very happy together. And who wouldn't when they're leading the fairytale life and expecting a new baby." How could such a sweet voice sound so cynical and accusatory?

"I need to speak to you privately," I said, ignoring her barbed tone. "You won't want your family to hear what I have to say. Do you mind if we close the door?"

She shrugged, acting too nonchalant, given the circumstances. "Close it if you like." She took a seat in a worn old chair.

I closed the door and took a seat opposite her. "We both know you spilled my pregnancy news to the press." I meant to make her defensive. "What I don't know is why you did it behind my back? I was willing to help you. I would have given you the story to sell if you'd just given me time to tell Riggins about the baby first and asked for the story."

Shock followed by triumph crossed her face. "Riggins didn't know?"

"Don't play innocent with me." I frowned at her, trying to maintain control of my anger. "Of course he didn't know. You knew he'd been gone since before I'd have suspected I was pregnant. Naturally I'd wanted to tell him in person."

She had the good grace to at least fake looking somewhat contrite. "Sorry."

I was sure she wasn't. "Did you get the money you needed?"

Her eyes narrowed. "We aren't evicted, are we?"

I raised an eyebrow.

"Barely. And just in time." She might have added, *No thanks to you.* She looked like she wanted to.

"But in the end it was all thanks to me, wasn't it?"

"Good. At least you got what you needed for all the trouble you caused." I paused. "You know I would have helped you if I could."

She didn't roll her eyes, but somehow made it plain she wanted to. "Really? You would have. You weren't too busy accepting multimillion-dollar knickers from your duke?"

Somehow I maintained my composure. "Don't tell me that story has made its way here now."

Nice move. She was clearly angling for the upper hand.

She pulled her phone out of her pocket, brought up a screen, and spun it around to show me. "When a duke buys underwear with a multimillion-pound swing ticket, the word will get out all the way over here. It's all over social media."

The absurdity of the situation hit me. I laughed. "One, I didn't have them when you asked me for money. And two, what would you want me to do? Pawn my panties?"

She smiled then. "Score one for you. But you can rest assured. The earldom is safe. For a few months, at least."

"Good. Because I want to make it clear I won't be as forgiving if something like this happens again." I didn't need Rose making a habit of selling my secrets for cash. Not without my permission, anyway.

She shrugged again. It seemed to be her signature move.

I took it as her way of agreeing. "As long as we're clear. And while we're making things clear, understand this, too. You can stop any further scheming to break Riggins and me up to get a share of the dukedom. My claim to the inheritance goes well beyond marrying Riggins. I'm the late duke's great-granddaughter, and I can prove it."

Rose's mouth fell open. I'd actually taken her by such surprise she had no retort. I thought she paled a little too as I explained a bit more about what I'd found.

"So you've come to put me in my place?" she said when I finished.

"I came to make my position, our relative positions, clear."

Her nostrils flared slightly. "If that's all—"

"That's not all," I said. "I require some penance on your part. Some restitution for all the trouble you've caused me. And if you're very good, I'll keep you in my inner circle and not ruin you. Invite you to all my parties. Introduce you to the right people. Basically, help you keep your celebrity circle and reputation up."

Her eyes narrowed. "What do you want?"

I paused, wanting her to feel my wrath, using my position of power to its full advantage. I wanted her to squirm. Not out of revenge, but because a person with Rose's personality needed to know unequivocally that I was boss and couldn't be pushed around or easily sucker-punched again. If I didn't flex my muscles now, she'd never respect me or stick to her part of the agreement.

"Information," I said slowly, meeting her gaze with a steely one of my own. "Double-cross me or go back on your word and you'll regret it."

Her answering gaze held a hint of respect. She expected a threat.

I paused again until she gave me a small nod of acquiescence.

I nodded back just perceptibly enough for her to see. "You grew up here. What do you know about our gamekeeper Bird, his late wife, and son? I want to know everything. And what you don't know, I want you to find out for me. Discreetly."

She laughed and clapped, clearly delighted. "Darling, Haley! I do believe you and I are going to get on." She paused. "What a delicious assignment. Where do I start?"

Riggins

Thorne was his usual jolly self when I met with him at his London office. Which was to say he was in his standard staid mode. It was raining in London. One of those days that reminded me of Seattle and made me homesick. But I had the feeling I was going to be trapped spending most of my time in England until I could convince Haley to come home with me. Damn that Dead Duke.

Even though I'd suspected it since the DNA test, I was still reeling from the revelation that Haley was, indeed, his full-blood great-granddaughter. Because of that one revelation, the Dead Duke's mania about his heir and an ancestor of Helen's continuing his dynasty made complete sense. He wasn't handing his legacy to a complete stranger. He was handing it to his bloodline.

I was furious about the situation. The more I thought about it, the more I realized I was the pawn in this whole grand scheme. It wasn't me who mattered, but Haley. She had to become duchess for his line to continue. I was just a means to an end.

Worse yet, I might never be able to pry her out of that damn castle. Then there was my inheritor guilt, if that was what you'd call it. Like survivor guilt. Why the hell should I inherit what rightfully belonged to her?

I had an obligation to do right by her now. And that damned obligation made any gesture I made, any action I took, look like exactly that, obligation, not love. And I was definitely in love with her. I couldn't even stay mad enough at her to stay away from her. She was constantly on my mind, invading my thoughts, making me burn with desire, filled with longing to laugh with her and share the intimacies of life.

What kind of douche would I be now if I cut her out of the estate? And yet there was no way to give it to her. And no way to stay married to her and divest myself of it. Now who was a prisoner of that cursed castle?

Then there was the baby to consider. I'd mentally been cursing the Dead Duke since Haley told me. He'd made damn sure I was never extricating myself from the almost royal mess he'd dropped me in.

"Congratulations, Your Grace," Thorne said, bringing me back from my thoughts to reality. "Tea?"

I shook my head. I was damned tired of tea. Why did no one ever offer coffee? "No, thanks."

"You must be overjoyed with the news." He smiled steadily at me, his mild expression completely in character.

He should be jumping for joy. He was successfully executing the Dead Duke's plan. If this child were a boy, no doubt Thorne would soon be getting some kind of performance bonus.

Hell, I deserved the performance bonus. I was the stud material here, and I meant that in a purely breeding way. I felt used. Like a horse put out to stud. Like a fool.

I resisted scowling at Thorne, trying to keep my anger and frustration to myself. "I'm hoping like hell it's a boy, if that's what you're referring to." I didn't want to give my true sentiments away.

"We all are, sir." He smiled wryly. "Then we can divest ourselves of the cumbersome requirements of the late duke's will."

"And your duties to play villain?" I grinned sardonically at him.

He didn't appear surprised at my mood. "You misjudge me, sir. I believe I actually enjoy the villain role. It adds spice and drama to my otherwise rather dull job. I'll miss it when it's over." He winked.

Okay, I hadn't expected such dry humor from Thorne. I cracked up. I couldn't help it. "You'd *have* to enjoy villainy to work for the Dead Duke for as long as you have."

Thorne shook his head and raised an eyebrow, but his eyes twinkled with humor and affection. "The late duke was misunderstood by most. Including you, sir, pardon me for saying. He was a kind and conscientious man at heart. The duchess appears to have a more accurate picture of him and sees him for who he really was." Thorne settled into the sofa across from me.

He had a comfortable grouping of furniture. Elegant and expensive leather. The Dead Duke had paid, and probably continued to pay, well.

"Speaking of the duchess—how long have you known she's the Dead Duke's great-granddaughter?" I watched his reaction carefully for any signs of surprise.

"Is she?" He nodded approvingly. "Well, we suspected as much, didn't we? It makes perfect sense, doesn't it, sir?" He looked like he was telling the truth.

He crossed his legs and studied me in return. "We both suspected, naturally, that the connection was closer than the story that she was a great-something niece of Helen's. Especially when the DNA test showed she must be directly descended from Helen herself.

"When I saw the duchess in person, my impression was strengthened. She looks a good deal like Helen.

But there's something almost indefinably Feldhem about her. If you knew the Dead Duke as well as I did, you would see it, too."

"What else do you know or suspect, Thorne? I need to know everything." I rattled off our suspicions about Bird and everything I knew about Bird, China, and Sid. "Is there any chance Sid is Bird's love child?"

Thorne considered a minute. "Very astute, sir. Of course there's a chance." He hesitated. "I told the duchess I thought her sister was a twin."

"Yes, I know. She told me." I frowned. "Do you think there's a twin? Could Bird have fathered twins with a Chinese girl and a son with his wife at around the same time? Could we be looking at a buffet of siblings that could match Sid?"

"It's possible." Thorne didn't look convinced.

"What other explanation is there? From what I've heard, Bird's son is Caucasian. Sid is a mix."

Thorne's brow furrowed. "Yes. That's always been a puzzle to me, too."

Neither of us seemed to have an answer.

"There's something else I need, Thorne. I need your legal assistance. I'd like to keep you on as my British solicitor with responsibilities for dealing with the castle and all aspects of the dukedom. You know it better than anyone. I hope that won't conflict with your duties as the Dead Duke's executor?"

"I don't believe so, sir. It's standard for a predecessor's competent solicitor to be kept on by the inheritor."

"Very good. Your first order of business is my will. If something happens to me, I want the castle and the entire Witham estate to go in its entirety to my oldest surviving child at the time of my death, whether that child is male or female. Enough of this male-centric inheritance bullshit."

Thorne raised an eyebrow. "Very good, sir."

I sighed. "Haley will be trustee and oversee it until the child is twenty-five. If I die with no living issue, the estate goes to Haley. In the case that she predeceases me, it goes to Sid.

"I'll make generous allowances for any other surviving children from my personal holdings and Flashionista."

Thorne grabbed a legal pad and pen from a nearby cabinet and took notes. "The oldest male child still inherits the title. A girl can't, not by law."

I nodded. "Understood. Of course, we're hoping this child is a boy." I laughed without humor. "Haley, naturally, will have her share of the Dead Duke's money to provide for her. My share will go toward maintaining the estate and providing for other children."

Thorne smiled knowingly, seemingly pleased with himself. "So there will be other children, sir?"

His question startled me. When I thought about it, I realized it sure sounded like I was planning a family with Haley. "Just covering all possible scenarios and eventualities."

"Very good." He asked a few more questions and made a few more notes. "I'll draw up the paperwork. Will there be anything else?"

"As a matter of fact, there is. What would happen to the estate and my title if my father suddenly showed up very much alive?"

Thorne looked up suddenly. He didn't appear as surprised as I expected he would. But he did look alert and maybe even slightly alarmed. "Your father was declared legally dead."

Nice evasive action, I thought.

"That's not the same thing as him really being dead, though, is it?"

Thorne didn't answer.

I wasn't accusing him of anything. But I also wouldn't have been surprised if the Dead Duke had gotten my deadbeat dad out of the way, clearing the path for Haley to marry me and become duchess. And that Thorne knew something about it.

It was just a theory. And maybe a crazy one. But there was no way Haley could have been induced to marry my father. Maybe he did drown after that boat capsized. Maybe he didn't. I wasn't about to go digging into it. But it was a contingency I had to plan for.

I shifted in my chair, leaning toward Thorne. "His body was never found. Would he have any claim to the title and estate?"

The ghost I suspected was haunting the tower was very human. I wondered...

"It's highly unlikely. If he did suddenly appear, it would open up a legal tangle for the title, perhaps." Thorne appeared a little too unconcerned. And slightly wary at the same time. "I wouldn't worry about it, sir.

You've been declared the duke and possession of all property was willed to you."

He paused as if taking time to compose his thoughts. "I would be leery, though, sir, of anyone coming forward trying to extort money from you for any reason regarding your late father. If someone appears purporting to know the whereabouts of your father, or makes any claims to the dukedom, you will let me know? Our firm has experience dealing with inheritance disputes and illywhackers."

Illywhackers? I hoped he meant con men. Whatever he was talking about, I had the feeling he knew more than he was letting on.

I nodded. "Of course." I wasn't going to let my suspicions show for the moment either. "Now that that's settled, do you happen to know which British firms handle and manage social media for the high-profile members of the British upper classes? I need someone to manage the duchess' media presence.

"There are American firms I have managing Flash's image. But I think the duchess could benefit from a British firm who knows the lay of the land here. I have one recommendation from a friend, but I want to be sure I'm getting the very best for the duchess."

Thorne smiled slowly. "I can connect you with a very reputable firm that's worked for various members of the royal family. Will that do, sir?"

CHAPTER NINE

Haley

"Bird's wife was a fat old cow," Rose said with a laugh. "No one in the village liked her, particularly. I didn't know her, of course, but I heard the help gossip about her. She held her position as the gamekeeper's wife over absolutely everyone. And was too proud of the house that came with the position for anyone's taste. She held that over people's heads, too."

"But Bird must have loved her?" I hoped. Otherwise her life seemed so sad.

Rose shrugged one shoulder and threw up her hands. "Heaven knows why if he did. She must have been decent looking and possibly decent-mannered at one time. How she produced such a handsome son is rather a mystery to everyone.

"Will Bird is smart, charming, and good looking. One of my younger sisters had quite the crush on him. Which was a bit scandalous. Papa is old-fashioned. He still believes an earl's daughter should marry up if possible."

Rose pulled her phone from her pocket. "Here. I'll show you his picture." She brought one up.

My heart raced as she handed me her phone. As I took a look, my hopes crashed. He *was* good looking. *And very white.* As I'd heard in the village. I saw no trace of anything vaguely Chinese about him. He had blond hair and blue eyes. He bore no obvious resemblance to Sid that I could see. None of her exotic beauty.

"Well?" Rose asked.

"Yes, very handsome." As I took another look at his profile, his birthdate jumped out. It was the same as Sid's.

My heart nearly stopped. How probable was it that Bird had three children born on the same day? One to his wife and twins to a mistress? Or could it be that the twin Mr. Thorne had heard about was Will? And was a twin only because he and Sid were both Bird's children and, by an odd quirk of fate, born on the same day?

Rose cleared her throat and gave me a funny look. "Are you all right? You look pale."

I nodded. She was probably afraid I'd throw up in one of *her* vases. "I'm fine."

She frowned slightly, not quite believing me, if her expression was any indication. "I can get you a cream cracker to settle your stomach. We have a box of them in the cupboard."

She was definitely worried. I shook my head. "I'll be all right." I let her think it was the pregnancy making me sick.

"If you're sure you're quite all right, Mrs. Becker is working out front getting the abbey ready for tourist season. She's from the village and about Bird's age. Also, a big gossip. Let's go talk to her. She may know something."

I followed Rose out.

Mrs. Becker was quite the talker. She took up Rose's story with ease. "How she produced a child *at all* after all those years of being barren is a mystery to everyone. Some suspect she didn't.

"She went to China and came home five months later with a beautiful blond baby boy. Raising speculation that she and Bird had adopted Will and were keeping the adoption mum. She was a proud, arrogant woman, and none too well liked. Some even say that Will was Bird's love child with another woman.

"If he is, no one would have blamed Bird."

That would fit well with what I had originally suspected. But made no sense now, because Will was white.

"Will was only a few weeks old when Mrs. Bird brought him home to England. She was so fat, that rolly kind of fat, it was hard to tell whether she'd ever been pregnant or not. You know the kind, I imagine."

Rose nudged me. I nodded.

Mrs. Becker laughed. "Well, maybe you don't. She was cute when Bird married her. Plump and curvy. But once she caught him, she let herself go.

"She and Bird weren't a good match, never were. After she had Will, they bonded over him and not much more. There was iciness between them for quite some years after Will was born. And right to the end, you didn't dare mention China to her.

"Something happened between her and Bird in China. We all think it was another woman."

Sid's mom?

After leaving Rose's, I had the car drop me off in the village. I spent the rest of the time before my appointment with Bird shopping and running errands. I loved the pleasant atmosphere and friendly people. It took my mind off the puzzles swirling around.

I arranged to have my purchases delivered to the castle. And even though the day was showery and breezy, I enjoyed the walk to Bird's cottage. Which wasn't really a cottage in the traditional sense, or at least what I imagined when I thought of one. It was a large, two-story brick house that looked larger and more posh than the home Sid and I owned in Seattle.

I could see why the late Mrs. Bird put on airs. It was grander than ninety-nine percent of the homes in the village. She should have had a large family to fill it. I wondered at Bird rattling around it all by himself. I wasn't good at guessing the size of buildings, but it had to be three thousand square feet or so.

I rang the bell, heart pounding. Bird answered so quickly, he must have been watching for me to arrive.

"Your Grace." He bowed his head respectfully. "Please. Come in, madam." He stepped aside to let me pass.

I still had a hard time being called madam or ma'am or your grace or duchess all the time. These days it seemed only Riggins called me by my name. And not often enough, instead choosing to use the teasing term "duchess" too often for my tastes.

The cottage was well lit and warm. A little too warm at the moment. I was flushed with the exercise from my walk.

Bird was an ordinary-looking middle-aged man. Gray hair that could have been blond at one time. Weathered. Blue eyes. Certainly not as handsome as his son. And only the barest trace of similarity to Sid. Something maybe in the shape of his face? In any case, it was so generic and faint that I couldn't immediately attribute it to him being her father.

"Nice of you to come, madam."

I followed him to a pleasant sitting room. All these old houses seemed to have them.

"Or did you want to look around?" he said uncertainly. "I've been out tracking the birds this morning. Looking for nests and seeing what kind of hatchlings we'll have. I haven't had much time to straighten up the place. The cleaning lady comes in tomorrow."

I smiled, trying to reassure him. "No, no. That won't be necessary. I'm mostly here to introduce myself and see if there's anything we can do for you. I should have come earlier."

"Oh, no, madam! I didn't expect you to come at all." He looked almost embarrassed. "The late duke, kind as he was to me, hadn't been to the cottage in over twenty years."

"Which is exactly why I've come! To make sure the house is in good repair."

"Oh." He brushed my concerns away. "Don't worry about that. The duke, I mean, the late duke, took care to keep the cottage up to date and well tended. I see to most of it myself and send the bills for any supplies or anything I can't manage myself and need to hire out to the estate. It's a good system. Same one as my dad before me had with the duke.

"If it doesn't inconvenience you and the new duke, I'd like to suggest we go on as before." He gave me a hopeful look.

I took that to mean he was highly private and independent. He didn't relish the thought of me, or Riggins, intruding in his personal domain.

I nodded softly. "That sounds good to me."

There was a pair of chairs near the fireplace. He offered me one, as well as tea and refreshments. I took the chair and declined refreshments. He took a seat in the chair opposite me.

I hesitated. "Actually, I lied. Partly, anyway. I wanted to talk to you away from the castle about more than the state of your home."

I paused again, trying to frame my words. "I came because you and your family have been on the estate for all of the late duke's reign. And I...I'd like to get to know him through your recollections." I took a deep breath. "This is strictly in confidence, but I recently discovered that he was my great-grandfather. It was a shock, but a pleasant one. I found documentation in his personal effects. I don't want to betray any more family secrets."

Fortunately, Bird didn't push for details. Or even appear more than passingly curious. I was suddenly glad for his quiet nature and apparent aversion to gossip.

"But I'm hoping you can help me. I feel like you knew him better than anyone."

If Bird was surprised, he didn't show it. Instead, he smiled largely and laughed loudly. "As you're the very image of the first duchess Helen, your news doesn't surprise me." He didn't quite wink, but it was clear what he meant. He could imagine how it had gone between the Dead Duke and Helen, and circumstances that could have led to me being the Dead Duke's granddaughter.

Bird studied my face. Finally, he nodded approvingly. "I didn't know the duchess, of course. I only know her from her pictures in the castle. But there's something about the late duke in you. It's not obvious at first glance, but if you look closely, it's there."

I grinned back at him. "You don't know how happy that makes me. I'm glad to hear it! I think so, too. Tell me everything!"

He shuffled in his seat. "*Everything*'s a tall order, madam."

I laughed. "It is, isn't it?" Especially since he wasn't really a talker to begin with. "Start with your memories of him as a boy. I heard he didn't like children."

We spent a pleasant half-hour reminiscing about Bird's boyhood and growing up on the estate with the Dead Duke at the helm. All the memories of the Dead Duke were pleasant ones, as far as I could tell. At the very least, Bird filtered his memories to share only the nice ones with me.

I was hoping he'd tell me about China.

"He loved the estate and the game. Very concerned about the game and proper management of it," Bird said.

I nodded. "Yes. I've heard that from others. He even sent you to China twenty years ago or so to learn some new technique?"

Bird tensed. "Yes. Indeed, he did. I was there nearly a year."

"I've never been to China," I said. "Was it wonderful?"

"It was. And it wasn't." He looked almost heartbroken. "My son was born in China. The duke was very helpful during that time."

My senses went on high alert. "Is that his picture on the mantel?"

"It is."

"I'd love a closer look. Do you mind?" I started to get out of my seat.

Bird jumped up and grabbed the picture, handing it to me with a proud look on his face.

It was a different photo from Will's profile picture. A younger Will. "He's very handsome. I heard he's away at university?"

Bird nodded.

"You must be proud."

"Bursting." Bird smiled.

Holding the picture, I turned to study Bird. "I have a sister about his age. She's adopted. From China." I told him the name of the province Sid was from.

No great surprise registered on his face. Just the mild look of someone who realizes they have something in common with you.

"That's where we were. Very pretty. Parts of it, anyway."

I nodded, smiling. "I'd like to see it sometime." I paused again, preparing my money shot. "Her birthday's coming up." I rattled it off.

"That's the same as my son's." Again, he spoke with only mild surprise and no apparent suspicion.

"It's an odd coincidence, isn't it?" I said, trying not to sound like I was accusing him of something. "Both of them having the same birthday and being born in the same province."

Bird laughed more heartily. "Not so much. There are a lot of people born in China every day, Your Grace."

To my disappointment, he didn't look guilty of hiding a thing. That my sister was Chinese and born on the same day as his son in the same village meant nothing to him.

It was clear he'd about talked himself out. I left his cottage shortly after. As I approached the maze, I swore I saw a figure dart into it. The hairs stood up on the back of my neck. Damn that Sherlock Holmes and his hounds of Baskerville for putting scary thoughts into my head. I was pretty sure no great big dogs were following me. But I had the sense that someone was.

I brushed it off as my imagination. Since the pregnancy announcement, Riggins had tightened security around the castle. The odds that a vagrant or stalker would be able to hang around the castle grounds unnoticed by our security team were slim.

I hurried back to the safety of the castle and the pleasant surprise of Riggins waiting to take tea with me.

He had a devilish look in his eyes as we sat side by side on the sofa in the drawing room and dined on British scones, which were much cakier and less sweet and rich than American scones. As a baker I took a professional interest in the differences. Slather them with enough jam and clotted cream and that made up the difference.

We discussed our day. I left out the part about being frightened as I walked by the maze. I wasn't even sure I'd seen anything.

He told me he'd hired me a press secretary of my own, someone to manage my appearances and handle my social media and any situations like Rose's leak to the press. It was sweet of him.

Every time I looked at Riggins, which was constantly, my heart squeezed. I wanted him to want to stay with me forever. I wanted tender words of love. And hot words of passion. I wanted to laugh with him. Lie with him. Love him. For the rest of our lives.

If this baby was a girl, I had a better chance of that. For a while, anyway. But we needed a boy.

As always, the tea was delicious. The look in his eyes as we finished was better.

"What?" I asked coyly. I was pretty sure what.

"You have a crumb on your lip." He leaned forward and kissed me. "We haven't done it in the drawing room."

"No, we haven't," I said, and slid into his lap. We still had dozens and dozens of rooms to go. "It's a rather obvious choice, isn't it?"

"But highly dangerous." He kissed my neck and played with my hair.

"As dangerous as the poison garden?" I ran my fingers through his hair.

"Infinitely more dangerous. Someone might walk in to clear away our tea." His lips travelled down my neck to the tops of my breasts.

"Bring it on."

The ice between us was truly thawed. If there had been any doubt about where Riggins would sleep, it was over now for sure. He slept in my bed that night. And all the nights after for a blissful week and a half.

We went to London to the theater. We toured the countryside and made plans for the estate. I even got him to look at baby things. But he couldn't stay in England forever. Flash needed him. He was called back to Seattle. He pressured me to go with him. But two days before we were supposed to leave, I got a bout of hyperemesis gravidarum, severe morning sickness that put me in the emergency room. I had to stay in the hospital overnight.

Riggins was right there with me. He wouldn't leave my side. But it was no way to bond. And there was also no way I felt like flying. The trip from England to Seattle was just too long.

He delayed his departure a few days until I was stable. But on April Fools' Day he went back to Seattle, leaving me in the capable hands of a private nurse, and the ongoing throes of morning sickness.

I was relieved, in a way, to see him go. I didn't want him to see me in this horrible sick state, constantly throwing up. It was debilitating. And embarrassing. And not conducive to romance or making him fall in love with me. I slept. I ate cream crackers, as the British called soda crackers. I threw up. I tried endless remedies. I prayed I'd be one of the lucky ones and the morning sickness would peak at some point between nine and thirteen weeks, as my doctor said usually happened, and not last the whole forty.

I let the nurse take care of me. Let Gibson run the household. Let our chef and Alice run the kitchen and Mrs. Rees clean the castle without instruction. I let Bird manage the game.

Everything ran on autopilot. It ran so well, I wondered if I was needed at all around the castle.

I was too sick to care about anything. I mostly gave up on my quest to find Sid's twin and whether Bird was her father. I felt horribly guilty about that. But I simply didn't have the energy or drive. Or five spare minutes where I wasn't tossing my cookies. First thing when I got through this, I promised myself.

As for Sid, she insisted on talking every few days, remaining upbeat and encouraging, and, as desperately as she needed and wanted a cure, not pressing me to do more investigating. She kept me informed on all the happenings in Seattle. Which made me homesick on top of being morning sick. But still, it was sweet. We made plans for her to be in England with me at the end of June after class was out. And in time for my twenty-week appointment, where we would find out the gender of the baby.

"We need a gender-reveal party," she reminded me. "I'll help you plan it." She clapped gleefully and maniacally.

She could get annoyingly excited about stuff. "You'll be announcing a duke's baby's gender. Boy? Or girl? The future of the dukedom is at stake...dum, dum, dum." She laughed as she made her joking, ominous sounds. "It will be an event. No, not just an event. *The* event. There hasn't been a baby born to the duke of the realm in nearly eighty years. Your gender-reveal party will have to be over-the-top grand."

I was so sick and tired I could barely work up energy for living, but her enthusiasm made me smile. I promised to include her. "Crap. This duchess stuff is overwhelming sometimes. All I really want is a simple gathering with you and a few of Riggins' close friends. If it's going to have to be on the scale of a wedding—"

"Oh, it will have to be," Sid said, enthusiastically ominous.

I made a snap decision. "Then I'm hiring an event planner."

Sid clapped again. "Brilliant! Can I ride roughshod over them? I've always wanted to boss an event planner around and make outrageous demands. This may be my only chance. Who knows when I'll get to be a bride?"

I rolled my eyes. She was so adorable sometimes. She could be bossy, but she was never mean. I seriously doubted making crazy demands was really a dream of hers. "You mean you want to be my maid-of-honor-type person for the gender reveal?"

"Exactly. I'm good at it, too."

She wasn't kidding. She really was. And I didn't have the energy anyway. "Done. You're it. I'll give you a budget."

"Hehehe."

"Are you twirling your mustache, Snidely?" I laughed.

"Absolutely. And I'm angling to be godmother to this kid, too. Someone has to be around to teach it how to party."

I laughed again.

My PR firm handled all inquiries regarding the current state of my pregnancy and how I was feeling. Why anyone should care, I didn't know. But somehow every time I threw up was newsworthy. And so was every millimeter the baby grew. Apps abounded that told you the size of your baby at every week of pregnancy. It's the size of a sesame seed. The size of a plum. *It's the size of a peach, honey!*

My PR team, however, wasn't satisfied with any of those mundane apps and their everyday generic descriptions. They put my growing baby's size into ducal terms and convinced Justin, who was a programming genius, to design a custom app to track Baby Feldhem's development. And any other growing baby whose mum wanted to track it in aristocratic terms.

We gave it away free on the website that Riggins established for the castle and dukedom. It was a hit. As was the betting pool to guess the date and time Baby would be born. My team had convinced Riggins to donate a large Flashionista gift card and cash prize. Which may have accounted for a lot of the popularity.

Riggins thought the whole idea was hysterically funny. Yeah.

So my baby, and anyone else's if they cared to use the app, was the size of a ducal seal from Riggins' signet ring. The size of the center diamond in the duchess' tiara. And on and on. When it reached the size of the castle wall, I was done for. Hopefully baby bun would be done before that.

And, in a case of strange bedfellows, Rose became my greatest ally. Maybe she was worried I'd go back on my word and this was her insurance against it. Whatever the case, she mentioned me as often as possible in all her social media, painting a flattering picture of me to be sure. She was a minor national celebrity and used that to our full advantage.

She played up her close social connection to me, spilling my "secrets," and making me into some kind of heroine for bravely bearing the trials of pregnancy with dignity. She managed to make my travails sound almost humorous. Where would the duchess throw up today? Nothing was immune from a sudden lost lunch.

I'd never had so much sympathy in my life. It seemed that hyperemesis gravidarum hit duchesses with startling frequency. To my great surprise and pleasure, I even got a wonderful note of encouragement from the princess.

As I had promised Sid, I hired an event planner for the gender-reveal party. And put Sid in charge, taking only a final-say role for myself.

Riggins. Even though we talked almost every day, I missed him so much I ached. I worried that I was losing my chance for him to fall in love with me. That he'd forget about me. Maybe most pregnant women are a little insecure about something. But for me, in particular, having a bun in the oven wasn't sexy. I was a mess and felt barely alive. There was no energy left over to feel even halfway attractive.

There was no point in Riggins being here. I knew he felt guilty that I had to bear this burden. But what could he have done besides hold my hand while I retched into the handiest receptacle?

No, it was better for him not to see me constantly like this. Better to wait until I blossomed in this pregnancy and had that famous radiant pregnant glow. That was what I told myself. But I couldn't help thinking it was a lie. And holding out hope that it wasn't.

Riggins promised to return for the big gender-reveal event that Sid had so well in hand. And had given me a generous budget for it. But although neither of us admitted it, we were both nervous about it. Me maybe most of all. Because a boy could mean the end of our relationship and free us both from the contract and the clutches of my great-grandfather. And a girl would be a disappointment and keep us under his control. Was freedom better? Or worse? Why was there always a downside?

It poured rain in April and May. Week after gloomy week of it until I dreamed of a tropical paradise and felt as if the sun had abandoned us forever.

Slowly, somehow, the weeks passed. The morning sickness hung on fiercely until about week eighteen. And then, a day at a time, it receded so gradually I didn't notice at first. One day I went an entire hour without throwing up. Then two. Then a whole morning.

I began to be able to keep food down an ounce at a time. Food began to smell good again. Then sound good. Then taste good and stay down. I started to gain some weight and look more and more like a pregnant woman. Not a dehydrated skeleton with a basketball shoved beneath her shirt.

I started to feel more and more like myself. I began taking an interest in life again. I started walking the grounds and the garden. And once again, I had that sense of being watched and followed. *It has to be the security detail,* I told myself.

But when I asked the security guys about it, they denied following me. They even showed me security feeds that proved it. And also proved I'd been alone. No sinister figures lurking behind me. On a few occasions, I took one of the security guys with me into the maze and the gardens. Nothing. No one.

No one on any of the security feeds. And yet I kept watching the Ghost Tower, looking for the light again. There were times I thought I saw something. But when I ran to the security room and asked them to check the cameras, there was nothing. And the Ghost Tower was always locked tight when we checked it.

It made me uneasy. I wanted Riggins. I felt safer and more secure when he was here. I even joked with him and asked him to borrow Lazer's ghost-hunting gear next time he came. I wasn't going crazy. I trusted my instincts. Something, or someone, was out there.

I busied myself planning for Sid's visit and Riggins' return. And bracing myself for finding out what I was having. Boy? Or girl? It was ridiculous how important that was.

CHAPTER TEN

June
Riggins

I'd been running. Literally every day. And metaphorically from everything else—impending fatherhood. That damn dukedom. My feelings for Haley. No matter what I did, or how hard I tried, I couldn't fall out of love with her.

Not when we talked via video chat and she looked tired and wan. Not when she was so exhausted and sick she lost her sense of humor. Not when she showed me her growing belly. Not when I lay sleepless and alone in my luxury bed at night. She was out of sight, but never out of mind.

Every little thing she did made me fall more in love with her. The notes she sent me. The stories she managed to tell me about castle life. The way she held up her blouse and pressed her pregnant belly to the computer screen so I could see the baby move. Or imagine I did.

Not when I saw the hell she was going through carrying my child and how bravely she faced it. Not when she'd be in the middle of a sentence and have to tear off to the bathroom.

She was trying so damn hard to make me fall in love with my unborn baby. It was cute. Damn. Why *did* I find that so adorable?

I read her social posts, full of humor about being pregnant and sick. Even though I knew her media team was managing them, they were somehow intimate and sweet. When it came right down to it, I loved everything about her.

Life would have been simpler if I could have gotten over her. It was a selfish thought, I knew. I kept hoping it would happen. And only grew more miserable at the thought of losing her.

As the gender reveal approached, I grew more and more apprehensive. I should have told her months ago when I flew to England to tell her the night I found out about the baby. Now I'd waited too long and found myself conflicted. How did I tell her I loved her now? In a song? Written in the sky? Blurt it out? Take her in my arms and tell her straight out, softly, intimately, *I love you.*

What if this baby was a boy? She'd get her bonus for having an heir. The Dead Duke would give her Sid's cure and she could walk. We both could. The thought of her leaving me tore me up. How would I live without her? I'd been such a douche.

A week before I left for England, my PI found something in China. He turned up a connection between Bird and Sid's biological mother. He had proof they knew each other. People who reported they'd been on very friendly terms. And something else—Will Bird was adopted. The Dead Duke had been instrumental in arranging it.

We had enough circumstantial evidence now to build a case that Bird was likely Sid's dad. But what we really needed was a DNA test. I held on to the information. I wanted to give it to Haley in person. This was something we needed to discuss.

Damn. This could all fall apart so easily. I had a gut feeling that I had to arrange for Sid to meet Bird. That if they met, Bird would see himself in her. That if I dropped enough hints and laid enough groundwork, he'd realize Sid was his daughter. Barring that...

Hell, I hoped I didn't have to be more obvious.

The gender-reveal party would be the perfect place to bring them together.

On another front, I was still trying to puzzle out how much the Dead Duke was controlling us from the grave. Haley's reaction to being pregnant and her claims that she was as surprised as I was that she'd gotten pregnant seemed genuine. She claimed she'd taken her pills. I'd seen her take them on many occasions.

The results came back from the lab—the pills were genuine. Not placebos.

Now, it was true that someone could have replaced one pill, one she'd already taken. But how would they have done that? And why not replace the entire pill card to ensure she got a placebo enough times for it to be effective?

Checking the pills had been a wild goose chase to begin with. Tampering with them had seemed like an improbable plot from the beginning. How could the Dead Duke have assured that Haley would get pregnant? Was she innocent, as she claimed?

The doubt. That damn lingering doubt drove me crazy. I wasn't big on faith. I liked fact.

Haley sent me a canister of Duke of Witham tea as a surprise. Something to remind me of her. And the castle. It was a diligent, if futile, attempt to make me homesick for a place I barely knew.

I didn't care for the stuff. I wasn't fond of tea in general. One evening in early June, a cold, rainy front came through. Though it had been unusually hot the last few Junes, it wasn't odd for June to be cool in Seattle. I was working late, as usual. I sat in my office overlooking Puget Sound, watching the raindrops splashing in the water and decided, what the hell? Now was as good a time as any for a cup of that damn tea.

I made myself a cup and Britished it up with milk. I was trying. I really was. One sip and I was about to lose my resolve to drink it. I was ready to toss it and make a cup of nice dark roast coffee. The aroma of the tea reminded me too much of Haley and how much I missed her. That had essentially been the point.

Jennifer, my office assistant, was working late with me. She'd stepped out for a minute to grab some paperwork I needed. She knocked on the door when she returned. "Boss? Got it."

I waved her inside.

"Something smells good in here." She inhaled deeply. "Is that tea?"

I groused and held up my cup. "It is." I wrinkled my nose. "Haley sent it over for me from the castle. She's trying to turn me into a Brit." I nodded toward my coffee machine and the canister of tea sitting by it. "Help yourself."

Jennifer loved tea. She took me up on my offer without hesitating and headed for the machine to make herself a cup of hot water to steep it in. I had half a mind to give the rest of the tea to her. I watched as she opened the canister and took a deep whiff of it.

"Mmmmmm...delicious." She scooped a large scoop of the loose-leaf tea into an infuser and dropped it in her cup. "This is a blend I haven't seen before."

"It's Haley's favorite. She drinks it all the time."

"What is it?" Jennifer was something of an aficionado.

"A special custom castle blend—Duke of Witham tea," I said sourly.

Jennifer laughed and got a look on her face like she was about to tease me.

"Don't say it! Don't even think it," I warned her. "I didn't name the damn stuff. Blame the narcissistic name on one of my predecessors."

"I wasn't going to say a thing, boss." She looked too apparently innocent to be telling the truth. "Just...irreconcilable differences already? A coffee man should never marry a tea gal."

She studied the tea in the canister and finally took a sip out of her cup. "Red clover. It's definitely heavy on red clover. The sweet honey flavor gives it away."

She squinted and smacked her mouth in that way people do when they're trying to figure out what they're tasting. She was trying to guess the secret ingredients. Which was typical for her.

Red clover meant nothing to me. Jennifer was a master gardener. She grew a huge variety of herbs and flowers in her garden. And was a bit of an herbalist as a hobby. She believed in natural remedies and liked to grow her own ingredients as much as possible.

"Makes sense," she said. "England has a lot of red clover." She took another sip. "This really is sublime. A very nice blend."

She was just begging me to ask her.

"Go on." I grinned at her. "You're dying to tell me. Red clover must have some medicinal properties."

She raised an eyebrow. "Oh, it's used for a lot of things." She tried to look modest about her knowledge of plants. And failed. "You find red clover tea in all the good health food stores."

She got a devilish twinkle in her eyes. "Women use it to control symptoms of PMS and menopause. Some even believe it enhances fertility. Which hasn't been proven, I don't think."

She paused. "Unless you're on the pill. You have to be careful with it then. Red clover tea absolutely negates the effects of the hormones in the pill. It's the equivalent of poking a hole in a condom. You'll get rid of PMS, all right. For nine months." She shook her head and laughed softly.

I paled. *Shit.* Haley drank it by the gallon.

"Riggins? Are you okay?"

"Fine." I stared at my cup of tea as if it were poison.

Or maybe it was absolution. I had no doubt that Haley didn't know there was red clover in the tea. Even if she had, I'd bet she had no idea what its properties were. Why would she? Mystery solved. Haley was innocent on all charges of conspiring to get pregnant. She'd been conned as seriously as I had. But she'd been smart enough to realize the extent of the Dead Duke's manipulation before I had.

I mumbled a string of curses beneath my breath. The Dead Duke had struck again. Damn, that man was diabolical. He couldn't have predicted how much Haley would love that tea. But he certainly could have left instructions to serve it to her at every opportunity. Just in case we'd decided to try to thwart his plans for an heir.

What other snares had the Dead Duke set? That was the question. And how was I going to tell Haley about the tea? How would I apologize for doubting her and accusing her of deliberately getting pregnant?

I couldn't wait to get back to her. I wouldn't say I'd given up fighting the Dead Duke's will. But I was less certain about fighting fate. If it demanded I love Haley, I would. And suffer the consequences and sacrifices that came with it.

I had to tell her this time. No more letting circumstance get in the way.

I chartered a private jet to take me to England, as usual. I invited Sid along. There was no reason for her to fly commercial when our schedules coincided.

I liked Haley's little sis. As close as she and Haley were, I was sure she knew of the difficulties between us. I expected she would be distant and cold to me. Surprisingly, there was little tension between us. Haley had said that Sid had one of the kindest, most forgiving souls in the world. I was beginning to believe her.

Sid's excitement and awe of flying on a private jet was cute and almost infectious. I'd taken the luxury for granted for a long time. She made me see how lucky I was.

Sid was Sid and full of her usual excited chatter. She talked incessantly about the gender-reveal party and how eager she was to become an aunt. It was hard to resist her enthusiasm.

"Haley's going to be the most perfect mom," Sid said after our dinner onboard the plane. "Look at me! She raised me all by herself since Dad died. And did a pretty good job, I'd say." She gave me her signature sunny smile and a pointed look.

"Good to know she can handle a teenager when the time comes," I said dryly. "But can she manage a baby?"

"You're a tough nut, Riggins!" Sid shook her head and waved a hand at me dismissively. "She's only four years older than I am. But she's been a little mother to me since my parents brought me home."

At the mention of her adoption, I hesitated, feeling guilty for knowing what I did and not sharing it with her. If she was going to be the pawn that drew the truth out, she had a right to know the moves I was about to make. Even before Haley did, I decided. I didn't think I'd get a better opportunity to talk to Sid. She'd handed me my opening.

"Speaking of your adoption...I have something to tell you. I haven't even told Haley yet. We may have found your father."

Her face lit up. She was full of questions. I told her everything I knew, including my suspicions that Will Bird was her half-brother and Bird her father.

When I was finished, she jumped up, threw her arms around my neck, and hugged me fiercely.

"You're brilliant! You're a genius, Riggins."

"I wouldn't go that far," I said. "We don't know for sure. It's just an educated guess—"

She kissed me on the cheek and returned to her own chair, glowing with excitement. "Haley and I have been trying to find the connection for months. She's been playing detective. Or she was until she got so sick."

I nodded. "I know. I wanted to tell her about this latest development in person. Which is why she doesn't know about it yet. It's all circumstantial. The question is—what do *you* want to do?"

She answered without hesitation. "Meet Bird and Will, of course! As soon as possible. And find out for sure."

I nodded. How could I stop her? If I were her, I'd want the same thing. "Just go carefully around Haley. She'd had you all to herself all these years. If she has to share you with a brother—"

Sid shook her head. "She has nothing to worry about there! She'll always be my big sis."

"Don't get your hopes up too high," I said. "There's still a good chance we're wrong."

"I know," she said soberly. "But this is the closest we've come." She broke into a beautiful smile. "Tell me about Bird. Is he a good guy?"

I shrugged teasingly. "He's a hell of a gamekeeper."

"But as a father?" She looked suddenly uncertain and expectant.

"You'll have to judge for yourself," I said as kindly as I could, sympathizing with her. There was still a part of me that wanted to meet my father. And give him hell. "Bird is a decent guy as far as I can tell."

Which was more than I could say for my late departed dad.

"Good," Sid said. "If he is my bio dad, he has a lot to live up to. My dad was the best." Her voice cracked.

I got out of my chair, put my arm around her, and hugged her. I was going to be a dad and influence a life. Someday my kid could be sitting around making a commentary about my fathering skills. The thought scared the crap out of me.

CHAPTER ELEVEN

Haley

I was like a kid waiting for Christmas as I waited for their car to arrive. When it pulled into the drive, my heart danced with joy. I dashed onto the front steps of the castle to meet them. I had a moment's panic—who would I greet first? The husband I missed beyond reason? Or the sister I'd give my life for?

Sid made the choice for me. She popped out of the car first and ran to me, nearly knocking me over as she hugged me. "Hale! Finally! It felt like I was never going to see you again. It's been *forever.*"

I was so relieved to see her looking healthy and strong that my knees nearly buckled. I knew her and the disease well enough to immediately recognize any signs of relapse. Which I'd worried she would keep from me, particularly while I was feeling unwell. But she glowed with beautiful health.

I hugged her with tears in my eyes. "Missed you, too. I have so much to show you and tell you and talk to you about." I looked over her shoulder as Riggins stepped out of the car.

As always, the sight of him sent my heart skittering off course. Since we met, it felt like it beat only for him. Like he really was my other half.

Our eyes met. There was that instant spark between us. We could both try to deny it, but it was there, as it had been from nearly the beginning. The baby in my womb leaped and fluttered.

"The baby's moving." I moved Sid's hand to my bump so she could feel the tiny movements that were only just becoming strong enough for the outside world to see and feel. But my eyes didn't leave Riggins.

He came to me in quick strides. He caught Sid by the arm and gently pried her loose from me. "Sorry, sis. It's my turn now. Husbandly privileges." He pulled me into a kiss that took my breath away.

I melted into him, kissing him back, startled and pleased by the passionate way his lips possessed mine.

"I missed you, duchess," he whispered into my ear. "More than I thought possible."

Just then, the baby decided to introduce itself to its daddy and kicked hard enough into Riggins' rock-hard abs that his eyes grew wide with wonder as he felt the tiny movement.

"Was that what I think it was?" He sounded as amazed as he looked at my blouse stretched tight over my belly.

I nodded and moved his hand to my bump where the baby continued to kick. "Someone's jealous."

"Someone sure the hell is." Riggins laughed and bent to speak to my bump. "Daddy's home, baby. You're going to have to share Mommy now." He paused, staring at my stomach. "This kid is strong. And ferocious."

I nodded. "Like someone else I know."

Riggins looked happy and tender. Maybe...maybe he could fall in love with our baby. Maybe he was already.

Riggins held my hand as I showed Sid into the castle and watched her eyes go wide.

"Wow. Seeing pictures is one thing," she said. "Seeing it in person is something else. This place is beyond awesome."

I nodded and noticed Gibson standing by, waiting to be acknowledged. "Sid, I want you to meet our butler, Gibson. Gibson, my sister, Sid."

Before I could say more, Riggins interrupted. "I'm sure Sid would like to freshen up after her trip. I know I would. Would you show her to her room, Gibson?"

"My pleasure, sir," Gibson said. "This way, ma'am."

Sid gave me a quick, questioning look. It was clear she felt fresh enough already and ready to catch up with me. I, however, knew Riggins' intention. Or hoped I knew, anyway. It was the same as mine. A celibate life was no way for a married duchess to live. Now that I was no longer sick all the time, my libido had returned with a vengeance. I wanted nothing more than to direct the force of my passion at the hot, desirable man by my side, the man who belonged to me for at least as long as the sex of our baby was up in the air.

Riggins took my arm. "The duchess and I have a lot to catch up on. We'll meet in the library for tea in an hour. Sound good?"

Sid nodded, reluctantly. She was outnumbered.

"Very good, sir," Gibson said, directing her to the prime guestroom down the opposite hall from our suite.

The guestroom location was a matter of architecture more than convenience. The walls of the castle were thick and privacy not so much a concern.

Riggins propelled me to his room with his hand, squeezing mine. He closed the door behind him.

We stood facing each other, panting, in heat, both of us. Our gazes held. I was looking for something. The same thing I looked for every time he looked at me. If I had previously tried to mask my feelings from him, I gave up now. What was the point?

I loved him desperately. I should have told him. If that made me look desperate or scared him away, so be it. The time for game playing was over. We were having a child together. Whether we wanted to be or not, we'd always be bound to each other by it. Whether we went our separate ways or stayed together.

I voted for together. I had from the beginning. I'd thought, so many times, that he was coming around, too. Now I stared openly into his eyes, letting my heart shine in them.

He looked at me, too, with his eyes wide open so that the depths of them were pure and honest. He took my face in his strong, tender grip and tilted my face to his, leaning in until we were inches apart. "I have something to tell you. Many things to tell you. Things I should have told you a long time ago. Some of them can wait. Some of them I had my reasons for keeping to myself.

"One thing you absolutely have to know now." He leaned his forehead against mine. "I've been a stupid fool denying what's been obvious for so long." He swallowed and took a deep breath. "I love you, Haley."

My heart nearly burst. Can joy actually kill you? Can you die from happiness? The way my heart was pounding I thought it was possible, if not probable.

As I opened my mouth to respond in kind, his kiss came down on mine. One hand slid behind my head as he held my mouth captive. Not that I was in any danger of trying to escape. I kissed him back with the full force of my delirious joy and wrapped my arms and my whole self around him. As much as was possible with the baby between us.

With the heat between us, the scent of his heady cologne mingled with my perfume. Riggins had a scent all his own. Strong, masculine, confident, elegant. Other men could wear this scent, but no other man could wear it exactly like this.

I sighed with happiness to be in his arms again.

His lips slid from mine to my neck as he pulled at the hem of my maternity blouse. "Show me my baby."

I grabbed the hem from him and pulled it up over the bump. My skin was already taut and stretched firm, and growing more so by the day. The baby, the tiny traitor, had gone suddenly shy and still.

I looked down at my naked stomach. "Baby's suddenly hiding."

Riggins' eyes were dark and wide with desire. "That's not the baby I meant." His words were nearly a growl as he pulled my blouse over my head and unfastened my bra. "This is my baby. You're mine. My baby. My lover. My wife. My heart."

He caught me in his arms and carried me to the bed, threw back the covers with one arm, and laid me back on the plush, expensive sheets. He stood at the side of the bed and began unbuttoning his shirt.

I slid out of the remainder of my clothes, watching as he undressed rapidly in front of me, his clothes joining mine in a pile on the floor. I should have been shy of my awkward new shape. My body no longer felt like my own. It was a daily stranger, changing before I got used to its new form.

As Riggins' gaze took all of me in, I boldly opened my legs for him. I wanted him so badly I almost thought it was possible to come just from the caress of his loving, heated look. My dreams of late had been full of him making love to me. Wet dreams so powerful I'd almost sworn he'd come to me in the night. I woke from them unfilled and desperate. As desperate as I was for him now.

He bent to kiss me between my legs. But I was too fragile and on the edge for that. One touch of his tongue and I'd be gone, and that wasn't what I wanted. I needed a full completion. The full intimacy of him inside me.

I caught his head and pulled his face up until he gazed over the edge of my stomach at me. "No. No. Not now. I can't wait. Come up here."

He was erect and ready. He didn't need a second invitation as I pulled him up and to me.

His hips, which would normally press against mine, now rested against my swelling baby bump. I guided him until he slid into me and groaned softly.

I took his face and pulled it to mine until we were eye to eye. I had to tell him and tell him now.

"I love you," I whispered. "More than anything. I want you more than anything."

He was braced above me, trying to keep his weight off me and the baby.

I grabbed one of his hands and rested it against my belly as I put my heart and soul into my eyes and voice. "I love you, but I come with this baby. We're a set." I waved my arm around the room. "I come with this castle and this legacy. I come with everything. I'm yours. We're all yours. But we can't be separated."

"Damn it, Haley." His voice was hoarse. "Do you have to talk so damn much and steal my thunder? I'm the one who comes with this bloody castle." He drove into me, hard.

I gasped with the force of his drive and closed my eyes.

"Open your eyes, Haley. Look at me. "I'll take your package deal, but only if you take mine. Deal?"

When I opened my eyes, he was staring intently at me. His expression was set. It was clear he knew what he was saying. His soul was bare in his eyes. He'd take the package I offered, the deal he'd been handed. He'd do it all for me. I just wished he were doing it for himself, too.

I stared up at him with tears in my eyes. "You want the dukedom?"

"I want you." He moved inside me, more gently this time.

"You're not playing fair." I stroked his face. "I don't want you to resent me—"

"How could I ever resent you, duchess? You're all I ever wanted." He thrust again, harder.

This time he didn't let up. We moved together, rhythmically, letting the love between us flow. I arched up to meet him, as much as I was able with the bulk of the baby.

His skin was hot against mine. I was hyperaware of him, feeling even the fine hair of his legs rub against my bare thighs. I was open to him and vulnerable.

I clasped my legs around him and let him take me away. We were on a journey together, he and I. It was magical. And adventurous. And filled with danger, like life was. But we were one now.

The bed rocked with our passion. The ancient headboard pounded against the sturdy wall that had witnessed this act through the centuries.

Riggins let out a low, guttural grunt. I followed him on the waves of pleasure, crashing and crashing until I cried out.

When it was over, he lay next to me, cradled me in his arms, and pulled the covers over us.

Why now? I wondered. Why had he confessed his love now?

The question must have been on my face. After a moment of companionable silence, he told me everything. Everything he'd found out about Bird, everything he'd told Sid on the flight over.

"I should have told you first." He looked genuinely apologetic. "But it's Sid's life. I thought she deserved to know, especially when the opportunity was handed to me as if fate was serving it up on a platter."

I nodded, drowsy and happy in his arms. "Yes, of course she does." We'd have to get up soon.

"Red clover tea," he said suddenly.

I opened my eyes slowly, still drowsy with the afterglow of love. I leaned up on one elbow and stared at him, smiling and amused. "You want tea now? Red clover tea? I didn't think you *liked* tea. I don't think we have any red clover tea."

"Oh, we have plenty, believe me." He took a strand of my hair, twirled it around his fingers playfully, and laughed. "It's the key ingredient in the family blend. Duke of Witham tea is packed full of it. Have you ever heard the villagers refer to the tea as enhancing fertility?"

I shook my head, amused he believed in myths. "No. And if I did, I'd think it was nothing more than an old wives' tale." I tried not to mock him, but I couldn't keep my amusement out of my voice. *I* was usually the naïve one.

His expression remained totally serious. "The old wives apparently knew their herbal remedies. And so does my assistant Jennifer. She's something of an amateur herbalist. She tasted the tea and immediately tasted the red clover.

"Haley"—he stroked my cheek—"red clover tea, and your love of it, is how the Dead Duke foiled our attempts at birth control. Red clover counteracts the hormones in birth control pills, reducing their effectiveness. Like a hole in a condom, is the way Jennifer explained it. Your great-grandfather tricked us. Using the very British ritual of tea."

My mouth fell open. The tricky old man. I knew he was behind it. But the method was ingenious. Like something out of one of the Agatha Christie novels from his collection in the library.

Riggins kissed the strand of my hair wrapped in his fingers. "I'm sorry I doubted you. I never should have accused you of trapping me."

His eyes were filled with guilt. And my question was answered. He trusted me enough now to profess his love because he knew I hadn't betrayed him. And my great-grandfather really was a maniacal genius beyond measure.

"I forgive you." I leaned down and kissed Riggins. "We've all been pawns in his game. But it's over now. What more can he do to us? He has nearly everything he wanted. And so do we."

CHAPTER TWELVE

Riggins

As much as I wanted to lounge in bed with my wife all day, we'd promised to meet Sid in the library for tea. Reluctantly, I slid out of bed, handed Haley her clothes, and began to dress. "How have things been since I've been gone? Do you still feel like someone's been watching you?"

Haley had been keeping things from me during our calls. I'd had reports from my security team that she'd been concerned that someone was following her. At times, she requested security guards walk with her into the maze and even the poison garden on her daily strolls.

She gave me a quick look. She clearly knew what I was asking. "The security guys have been talking."

"Don't blame them. I demand daily reports." I paused. "You've still been feeling uneasy? Even after I added extra security details? I'll have more cameras and motion sensors installed."

She paused and nodded slowly. "I have. Maybe it's just my imagination. This place is rather gothic. And both lovely and scary when you're gone."

"Or maybe the ghost stories are true." I squeezed her knee.

She slapped my hand away. "You're mocking me."

"Wouldn't dare." I slipped into a T-shirt and tossed the button-down shirt I'd worn on the plane onto a chair to throw in the laundry later. "Any more ghost sightings in the tower?"

I would have laughed like I was joking, but I was half serious, maybe more.

She shook her head. Hesitated. And corrected herself. "Maybe. There have been a few times I thought I saw something."

She shrugged. "But I couldn't be sure. I checked the tower several times. It was always locked. The security team has orders to stay out of it, and I'm the only one with the key. There couldn't have been anyone there. But if it's a trick of the light, I can't figure it out."

I nodded. "Yes, well, maybe we *will* have to call those ghost hunters out."

With that, we got ready and met Sid in the library. She was bouncing with energy and eager to see everything, including Bird.

Haley was apologetic. "He had to run to London to pick up his son. Will's been on vacation in Europe with some buddies since school ended on the tenth. He was supposed to be back yesterday, but he decided to spend an extra day at a friend's house. They'll be back late tonight."

Haley knew why Sid was so eager to meet them.

"Give them a day to get settled in before we spring you on them," she said to her sister. She sounded as eager as Sid. "We need to plan carefully for all contingencies." She was smiling, but worry edged her expression and tone.

We could be wrong in our assumptions. Or right but Bird and/or Will could reject her. Neither of them was under any obligation to either acknowledge her or donate marrow. A ripple of tension filled the air.

Sid's returning smile was gracious. "You're right. I've waited a lifetime. What are a few more hours?"

I glanced between them nervously, hoping they wouldn't be disappointed.

Our conversation about ghosts was still on my mind late that night as I sat in the dark at the small desk in Haley's room and worked on my laptop. Jetlag was a bitch. I never managed to avoid it, no matter how many preventatives or remedies I tried. The pregnancy and excitement had worn Haley out. She stayed up as late as she could, barely eleven, then fell into bed exhausted. She slept soundly in bed while I worked.

I had a hard time keeping my eyes, and hands, off her. My heart was filled with the knowledge she loved me. And guilt for my half-assed answer about the dukedom. I was, apparently, stuck with it, so what did it matter if I actually wanted it?

But it seemed to matter to her that I did. I knew her feelings all too well—she didn't want us to be the duke and duchess who lost it. She'd read something in the Dead Duke's papers that she'd taken to heart: *The obligation of each new duke is to leave the dukedom better off than when he took possession of it.*

A fine sentiment. A nice ideal. But that meant increasing the value of the estate by a minimum of the forty percent estate tax just to leave it in the same shape as it was when he inherited. No small feat in the current economy.

Stiff from sitting, I stood and stretched. I walked to the window to clear my head. It was a clear summer night. My gaze naturally went to the Ghost Tower. It was dark and imposing. *Dark* being the operative word. As I rolled my neck, preparing to return to business, a light flickered in the upper window of the tower. It was very faint, but definitely real.

I pulled my phone out and snapped a picture of it so I could pinpoint the location later. Before I could make a move, it was out. I swore beneath my breath and looked back at the bed where Haley still slept soundly. Ghost or no, I was going in after that haunting bastard. Something was going on in the tower and I was going to find out what.

I put on a pair of tennis shoes. On my way out I stopped by the duke's suite and grabbed the key to the tower. And the ghost-hunting kit I'd ordered and stored on my last visit—a flashlight and night-vision goggles. Maybe I should have grabbed a silver stake or stopped by the kitchen for a head of garlic. I was a bit more prosaic and grabbed a hunting rifle. The foe I was facing was in all likelihood human and very much alive.

The midnight air was cool as I left the castle and put on my goggles. The grass of the lawn damp and heavy with dew. The hair on my arms and neck stood up from the chill. My stomach burned with excitement and my heart raced. I wasn't exactly afraid. Not of the usual things.

My heart beat heavy in my ears as I let myself into the tower and glanced at the picture on my phone, trying to pinpoint the location where the light had been. I raced up the narrow, circular staircase.

The tower had been designed as a fortress to be defended by the castle's knights, who'd been much shorter and smaller than modern men. As such, the staircase was tight and designed so that defenders familiar within the building could charge down the stairs with their swords drawn in the right hands, facing intruders whose right-hand swing was broken by the stone walls. Which put invaders at a disadvantage, especially in an era when it was considered unlucky and unnatural to be left-handed.

Wanting to catch my ghost by surprise, I didn't flip the lights on. Instead I relied on my goggles. I swung out of the staircase on the third floor and raced to a small stone room that faced Haley's window. The door to it was open as I approached.

I raised my rifle to my shoulder and stepped inside. A man was seated in the dark in the corner, casually eating a sandwich.

He set the sandwich down on a piece of butcher paper beside him, dusted the crumbs from his hands, and flicked a lighter on, illuminating his face. "Hello, son. I was wondering when you were finally going to realize I wanted to see you."

Haley

I woke suddenly, startled awake by a breeze. Or so I imagined. I was used to sleeping alone, but even so, I missed Riggins and his delicious hot body and heat. When I'd fallen asleep, he'd been working on his laptop at the desk.

I rubbed my eyes and sat up. His chair was empty now, but the laptop was still open and on. I glanced around the room, thinking he'd probably just gone to the bathroom. But my bathroom door was open and the light off.

"Riggins?"

I slid to the edge of the bed and slipped into my slippers and robe. Gibson claimed it was cool in the castle even in the heat of summer. And the heat of summer was still some time off. The chill persisted. I pulled the robe tightly around me and hugged myself as I went looking for him in his room.

His suite was empty, too. I went back to mine, working up the courage to go looking for him in the rest of the castle. Had he decided he wanted a midnight snack? It was the appropriate hour for it.

I didn't know what drew me to the window, but something did. I peered out, half expecting to see him taking a midnight stroll. The lawn was empty. But the light was back in the Ghost Tower, very faint. Just a flicker. But it was there.

No.

I knew exactly where he was. I didn't bother to look for the key. I was sure he had it. I took off after him.

Riggins

"Are you going to stand there in the dark looking like you've seen a ghost?" My derelict, and decidedly not dead, father got casually to his feet, surprisingly limber for a man his age.

He spoke with a strong British accent. Which I found startling and surprisingly foreign. All my life I'd known he was British on an intellectual level. But somehow, in my mind, whenever I imagined meeting him, he always sounded American.

If I'd been raised British, or had been a linguist, I could have told where he was from and what kind of accent it was exactly. To my American ears it was simply middle-class British. Not aristocratic on the one side. Not Cockney on the other. He was taller than I expected. His voice deeper, with a tone that women would find sexy. I hated to admit it, but I could see how Mom would have been attracted to him.

I hated him, but even I had to admit he had magnetism. At the same time, he was just as cocky and arrogantly confident as I expected from the little I knew of him. And irritatingly charming in a roguish way.

He was a good thirty years older than the picture my mom had kept on her dresser all those years, but still slender and fit. Still had a thick head of graying hair.

His face was lined with hard living, but, as much as it galled me, he was still a good-looking man. Even with the bags beneath his eyes. His face had lost the slenderness of youth and filled out. It had also lost the defined edges and was beginning to sag. He was on the border of developing jowls, but somehow that only made him look mature and distinguished. He had the distinctive and arresting Feldhem eyes. I looked too damn much like him for comfort.

I reluctantly dropped the rifle from my shoulder. I'd dreamed of punching the shit out of him since I'd been small. Now that I had my opportunity, I restrained myself.

"Hello, Dad. If I look like I'm seeing a ghost, it's because I am. You're supposedly dead. What are you doing haunting the Ghost Tower? It's a bit clichéd. Are the gates of hell open now? Is there a demon's holiday I should be aware of?"

He laughed. "Nice to see you, too, Riggins. They told me you had a sense of humor."

He may have found the whole thing funny, but I was chilled to the bone. His sense of timing was impeccably off. I hadn't wanted this damn dukedom in the first place. But now that I had it and a child on the way, I sure as hell didn't want to hand it over to this reprobate loser to destroy. And have to watch him do it.

He looked past me over my shoulder. "You must have been expecting me. You came alone. Or will security be here any minute?"

He was perceptive.

"Not until I call them."

"You wouldn't want to do that." He held the lighter up to my face and frowned. "You have me at a disadvantage. Take the goggles off so I can see you."

I flicked my flashlight on and pulled the goggles off, less out of consideration for him and more for comfort. I let them hang around my neck as he closed the lighter.

"I assume it's safe to have a light on here?" I said.

He shrugged, studying me closely and smiling. "As safe as anything." His expression softened as he examined me. "You look like me. But there are traces of your mum in you."

"Don't mention her. Don't talk about her. Don't pretend you cared about her." I refused to tell him she'd longed for him until the end. I refused to let him know he'd broken her heart.

"Ah, it's that way, then, is it?" He nodded. "It's good you're defending your mum. I'm sorry she's gone."

Maybe he was, but only in a peripheral, abstract way. I changed the subject before I gave in to my desire to take a swing at him. "How long have you been hanging around here? You're scaring Haley. And how have you managed to avoid the security cameras and security details?"

"Sorry to upset my beautiful daughter-in-law. That wasn't my intention. She's very perceptive. I only wanted to see her and my boy." He winked. "You know the answer to your first question." He sounded amused. "Since your honeymoon."

There was a chill in the tower. It crept down my back at the thought of my father watching our every move. And yet I had suspected it for some time. "And the security cameras and guards?" I paused. "You obviously have a key to the tower. But how did you get past security?"

He shrugged. "It was part of the deal the Dead Duke gave me to disappear. I can come home to this place any time I like, as long as I'm not seen. As you say, I have a key to the tower. And I know these grounds as well as anyone. The late duke made sure of that.

"He arranged the security cameras so that they have blind spots and I can avoid them at will. He gave me the plans and arranged the security details to leave me alone.

"This tower, with its history and its hauntings, is the perfect hideaway for a dead man like me. It was easy enough for him to order the tower locked at all times. Who would want to visit a haunted tower, anyway? Only the bravest.

"Everything was fine until you came along and started playing havoc with the security teams, changing things up, and making it more risky for me to stay here."

"You're not afraid to stay here?" I was curious.

"With the ghosts?" He laughed again. "I'm no coward. And not afraid of the supernatural. This place is nothing more than a creaky old building."

"It's not exactly homey."

"This room isn't part of my main quarters. There's a secret room accessible only by a hidden door. It was built as a place for the duke and his family to hide. That's where I live when I'm here. It's windowless, but quite comfortable. Fully plumbed. With Internet access and electricity. All I need now is for you to call off all this extra security you've been adding."

I stared him down. "Not so fast. What do you want?" I clutched the rifle tightly. "Money? Or are you here to claim the title?"

His booming laughter echoed off the walls. "No thanks, Your Grace. The title's all yours, you little American shit," he said affectionately.

"Good to hear, you old British bastard. You haven't answered my question."

"There was a time when I was young and impressionable that I could picture myself as lord of the castle, sure enough. Until it was explained to me by our late predecessor how my life would be if I didn't step aside. The late duke was never keen on me inheriting this beautiful estate. Though I can't imagine why." He laughed robustly.

"The bloody controlling old man." He shook his head, but it was as if he was mocking himself. "Once he laid it out, and detailed the responsibilities, I didn't want the dukedom after all. Like father, like son."

I balled my fist, trying to control my temper. We weren't alike at all. I had never wanted the dukedom. Nor even known it was going to be mine. He had wanted it at one point for its treasures. I didn't want it because of the obligation.

"The old Dead Duke—isn't that what you call him?—made it clear that I'd be left with an albatross around my neck and not much more. He didn't trust me with his legacy. Or cash."

"On that point we agree." I shifted the rifle.

"But he trusts you. He wouldn't have left me a penny to enjoy." His eyes sparkled maliciously, filled with jealousy and envy. "He left things to you all neat and tidy, though, didn't he, son?" He scoffed. "As if *you* needed *more* money."

"I earned what I have," I said as evenly as I could, trying not to let shock and anger get the best of me. "You sure as hell didn't leave me anything or give me a grand start in life."

He didn't have the good grace to flinch. He'd left Mom and me in dire straits. She'd scrimped and barely eked out a meager living for us my entire childhood. And all the while he'd been the heir to a fortune. I wondered if Mom even knew about it.

"As for me—the Dead Duke blackmailed me into taking the title and estate. I never wanted it." Until now.

Being reminded of my childhood gave me clarity. Haley was right—I had no right to squander our child's inheritance. It was up to them to decide what to do with it.

My father raised an eyebrow. "You don't want it, you say? If that's true, why didn't you bring security with you?

"You don't seem particularly surprised to see me. And you obviously weren't expecting a dangerous intruder or you'd have sent security to handle it. Could it be that you're afraid you'll lose the castle and title if it's discovered that I'm still alive?"

His accusation hit too close to home. I didn't want him to be discovered. Not yet. We had unfinished business.

I pointed an accusing finger at him. "And if you wanted the title only, you'd have gone public as soon as the Dead Duke died and staked your claim. If you don't want the title, you must want money."

"You don't give me much credit." He shook his head. "You disappoint me, duke. I thought you were brighter than that. How do you think the Dead Duke got rid of me?"

It was apparently a rhetorical question. He answered before I could open my mouth to respond.

"He made it worth my while. And ensured I didn't burn through my payout. I have enough to last until I die and live quite comfortably. It's doled out as an allowance. But you can't have everything." He laughed again. "The old man didn't trust me to manage my own finances any more than he did to manage the dukedom."

I didn't respond. On this point the Dead Duke and I were in total agreement. My father would have lost the estate within a year at most.

Thorne must have known about this arrangement between the Dead Duke and his true heir. Which was why Thorne hadn't denied that my dad was still alive.

His attitude and manner had all but warned me to back off the matter and let sleeping secrets lie.

"No matter," dear old Dad said. "I won't live *much* longer. Not long enough to cause you terrible trouble, anyway." He sounded surprisingly amused. "Since my time on this earth grows short, there's no reason to take the title away from you. It will be yours in a few months anyway. Well before the courts can make any sense of a dead man coming back to life." He clasped my shoulder.

I shook his hand off and jerked away from him. What did he expect? Whether he was really dying or not was of little relevance to me. As far as I was concerned, he was an unpleasant stranger. I had only the natural sympathy any person has for someone who was dying.

Reading my face, he sighed. "If it's all the same to you, I'd rather remain dead. It's much more fun. I can haunt this place at my leisure."

I stared him down, fighting my warring emotions. If he really was dying, I should have felt more compassion for him. Or at least checked to make sure the condition wasn't hereditary. As it was, I wasn't certain this wasn't another scam. "If you don't want money, why *are* you here?"

"Isn't that obvious?" His gaze held mine. For once he looked completely serious. There was something desperate in his eyes. "I wanted to meet my grown son, my only child. My legacy. Make my peace with you. Once I'm gone you'll be all that's left of me, Riggins.

"For a while, anyway. Until my grandchild is born." He paused, suddenly thoughtful and contemplative. Finally, he sighed. "I've never been much of a father—"

"You haven't been one at all—"

He held up a hand to silence me. "True enough. But in my middle age, I find I have a strange desire to know my grandchild and pass on a few life lessons. Fate is going to deny me that. The best I can do is meet my grandchild before I go. I want your word you'll let me see the baby."

I bit my tongue to keep from exploding. When negotiating, especially with a family terrorist, never show your weakness.

He laughed softly before I could answer. "I see myself in you. Conniving must be hereditary. You're trying to puzzle out how to outwit me."

I wasn't flattered.

"You don't want me to see my grandchild. That's plain enough to someone like me. What are you afraid of? I don't have enough time left to corrupt the little bugger."

"I don't owe you anything." I tried to swallow my anger. It left a bitter taste in my mouth. "I have no reason to trust you to keep your end of the bargain."

He stared me down. "No, I suppose not." His grin was quick. "You don't think I've reformed. I can't say as I blame you. I'm not sure I have, either. But running out on a grandbaby is different than deserting a son. A grandchild isn't the same responsibility, but it is my second and last chance at making things right."

He paused. "It's a fair bet you'll be making. You agree to let me see the baby. I agree not to make myself known. If the doctors are right, you'll never have to pay out on your end of the bargain. They don't give me more than a few months."

He shook his head. "My doctors scolded me for hard living and blame it on that. The smoking and drinking. The womanizing, maybe, too." He sighed, shaking his head again and wearing a small smile. "Those pompous medical professionals have warned me that my heart may not be strong enough for sex. If that doesn't sound like a commercial for male enhancement drugs—" A fit of coughing mixed with laughter clipped his words.

I didn't find it uproarious at all.

He pulled out a tissue and wiped his mouth. "Warnings won't stop me. I'd rather die in the act than abstain." He winked. "If sex doesn't kill me, I have advanced, incurable lung cancer and cirrhosis of the liver. One of those will do the job for you soon enough. I can't go back on my word even if I want to. I don't have enough time left."

I didn't give a damn about his health, except to hope he wasn't lying about dying. "It's a comfort to know I can always kill you with a well-timed visit from a prostitute. I always knew sex could be used as a weapon, but this is a little extreme."

He laughed. "I see you have my wicked sense of humor." He paused and became serious. "Promise me I can see my grandchild, and I'll stay dead until I really am."

Haley

I hurried to the Ghost Tower to confirm my suspicions. The outside air was chill and the grass and ground cold through my thin slippers. I clasped my robe tightly at my neck as I ran toward the tower.

It wasn't easy running with the extra weight and girth of the baby. I felt strangely off balance. My body was growing too fast for me to get used to my new shape at any given moment. As I ran, or maybe jogged was a better description, I held my baby bump with one hand, feeling like my baby was sloshing around in there. One thing was certain—I didn't have world-class running form.

I was breathing hard by the time I reached the tower. And was warm and flushed from the brief bout of exercise. My heart stopped as approached the door and found it flung wide open.

I hesitated on the doorstep, listening and trying to hear as my heart galloped back into action and my hands trembled. I'd come woefully unprepared to meet either human or supernatural foes.

I glanced around, looking for a weapon, and found only a few pebbles. If I hadn't been panicked, I would have laughed at the absurdity of thinking I could fend off anybody with a few pieces of gravel.

The baby kicked, reminding me I had more than myself to think about. I gasped and leaned against the outside wall. There was only one thing to do.

I pulled my phone from my pocket and called security. "The door to the Ghost Tower is standing wide open." I sounded both breathless and desperate. "Come immediately. But be careful. I think the duke may be inside."

A security camera over the door moved until it zoomed in on me.

"We have you on camera. Stay where you are, Your Grace," the guard in the control room said. "I'm sending help."

I hung up. Of course, I probably should have done as he said. But Riggins was in there. What was he up to? What if he needed me? What if he needed help now?

I slipped inside and stood in the main room, listening for a clue. At first I heard only the frightening sounds the tower was known for. The creaks and groans of age. The musings of the ancient stone walls that heightened its reputation for being haunted.

I was about to call out when I heard, very faintly, echoes of voices volleying down the stairwell. Two male voices, to be exact. One of them was Riggins'.

I restrained myself. What if this other man was dangerous?

I took a deep breath to give me courage and quietly mounted the stairs. The stone stairs were worn smooth and slippery, grooved and sloping in the centers from the thousands of footsteps they'd borne. Rutted like roads that needed resurfacing.

I slipped once or twice on the narrow wedges that wound around, catching myself in time and proceeding more cautiously. My slippers had slick soles, which made for slow progress in the first place. I kept one hand on the wall, clutching the stonework as well as I could for balance. I made a note to have a handrail installed.

I followed the voices to the third floor. As I approached, I saw light spilling as if from a flashlight into the stairwell and the voices grew loud and heated. There were no halls in the tower. All the chambers were directly off the stairwell.

I hid just outside the large chamber, listening and trying to get a peek at what was inside without being seen. Riggins had his back to me. The other man was obscured from view.

"Are you blackmailing me?" Riggins' voice was hard and angry.

"I prefer to think of it as cutting you a deal," the other man said. He sounded almost amused. And confident he'd get his way. His voice was deep with middle age. "I may not have been much of a father, but I did die for you. Remember that. You owe me something."

Father? My mouth fell open and went completely dry. I tried to remember what Riggins had said about his dad. I thought he was dead. Of course he was dead! Otherwise Riggins couldn't be the duke.

"Died for me?" Riggins snorted. "You faked your death for profit."

My heart raced. If Riggins' dad was still alive, Riggins wasn't the duke. This whole thing, everything we'd done and been through, was for nothing. His father would destroy the dukedom before Riggins inherited it. It was mine. My family legacy.

My mind raced, but I couldn't think straight. What should I do? What did I dare do?

"Semantics." Riggins' dad wasn't backing down. "What will it be? Is taking revenge on your old dad and denying him his last wish worth your birthright and a dukedom?"

My heart beat so loudly in my ears I could barely hear anything else. I shook so badly I had to hang on to the wall. I waited breathlessly for Riggins' response. My heart was so loud I marveled that it didn't give me away. I stood poised, ready to rush in and intervene. Ready to promise Riggins' dad anything he wanted if he would leave and leave the dukedom to Riggins.

"You arrogant bastard." Riggins' voice was hard. "This dukedom is mine. For Haley. For my baby. For *myself.*"

Tears filled my eyes. How was it possible to be ecstatic and frightened at the same time? *Riggins wants the dukedom.*

"You have a deal." Riggins' voice was still as sharp and hard as a polished steel blade.

I slumped against the wall, my knees weak with relief. Riggins' response was the answer to a prayer. The granting of a wish. And then I remembered that security was on its way. That I had quite possibly called down the destruction of everything the Dead Duke had set up and planned for us. Destroyed what I'd so desperately come to love.

The baby kicked again, once again taking me by surprise. I let out a small noise.

"Who's that?" Riggins' father moved toward the door.

I stepped out of hiding and into the doorway.

"Haley?" Riggins took a step toward me.

"There's no time. We have to hide your dad. Security will be here any minute."

CHAPTER THIRTEEN

Haley

The two men stared at me in disbelief. Riggins' dad actually got a soft, emotional look on his face as his gaze travelled to my baby bump.

The sound of a car racing toward the tower made us all jump.

"That's security!" I gave the men an entreating look. "I'm sorry. I called them. I didn't know." I glanced around frantically at the bare room, looking for something, anything to hide a man in. "We have to hurry!"

Why didn't anyone else feel my sense of urgency?

Riggins pulled me to him and crushed me against his chest. "You're freezing. You shouldn't be out in the cold like this."

"I'm fine. Or I will be once we hide your dad." My voice broke. I loved Riggins beyond reason. We were on the verge of our happily ever after. He wanted the dukedom! He wanted us. I wanted him. What more could I ask for?

Riggins' dad swore. "Bloody security. The bane of my nonexistence." He winked at me. "Nice to finally meet you, daughter." He nodded toward my baby bump. "May I? I'd like to feel my grandchild. This may be the only chance I get."

Riggins scowled at him. But I had sympathy for his dad. If he'd made a mistake with his son, he at least deserved a chance to make it up to his grandchild. I wanted to be able to tell my baby that his only living grandparent had wanted to hold him or her. I wasn't going to be the one who denied this dying man his wish or ruined the story for the future.

I pulled away from Riggins and presented my growing belly for him to touch. His large hands were warm and gentle as he cupped my belly.

"The baby doesn't move often—"

And then, just on cue, the baby kicked as fiercely as it ever had. I gasped. But the look of wonder on Riggins' father's face as it he felt it move was something I'd never forget.

He squeezed my belly as if hugging the baby, leaned down, and cooed to it softly. "There, there, my little duke. Nice to meet you."

"We don't know it's a boy." I rubbed my baby bump.

He straightened. "You're carrying low. Just like Riggins' mum did. It's a boy, all right."

Outside the tower, a car door slammed, the sound magnified in the still night air.

"There's a way back to my hiding room that avoids all the cameras." Riggins' dad nodded toward the staircase. "But I need you two to cover for me while I escape. If I'm caught, I'll make up some story about being a long-lost relative of yours." He winked again, still almost amused by the adventure.

I thought that given a chance, I might have liked him. He had Riggins' charisma.

"Good plan." I nodded and turned to Riggins. "Call the security control room and tell them everything's okay and under control. That you couldn't sleep and decided to explore the tower. I'll go downstairs and talk to the security guys that are already here and send them away. If I hurry, I can meet them at the entrance."

I turned and dashed into the stairwell without waiting for a response. My feet were on the stairs. Down, down, the spirals, taking them as fast as I could.

"It's all right!" I called out to security. "We're fine."

I rounded another corner. The steps were farther apart here and worn completely smooth. I misjudged and caught the edge of a step with the toe of my slipper. My foot slipped. My balance was already off. The sudden surge of forward momentum propelled me before I could catch myself with the wall.

I floundered, trying to get my balance. Where was the wall? *Where was the damn wall?*

I tumbled forward. My scream pierced the air. Instinctively, I wrapped my arms around my belly, trying to shield my baby. I hit the cold stones arms and belly first. "Riggins!"

My head hit something. I felt dizzy and disoriented. Unable to right myself, I tumbled. And tumbled, screaming.

Someone else was screaming and calling my name. There were footsteps on the stairs behind me. I tumbled end over end, bouncing off the walls. Banging my head again and again as I kept my arms wrapped around my baby. Banging my body.

My thoughts were jumbled. I was too surprised and shocked to feel pain as I kept falling and falling. My vision narrowed to a small tunnel. My ears rang, drowning out the commotion around me.

I hit the floor at the bottom headfirst. The tunnel grew narrower. The ringing louder. I could barely breathe. *Riggins.* I wanted Riggins. I tried to form his name.

There was a beam of light. Someone was standing over me.

"I'll take care of her. Go!"

Riggins. Thank goodness. Riggins.

"Run, man, run! *Hide,"* he said. "It's what she would have wanted." His voice was firm and desperate.

Suddenly there were arms around me. I was chilled and shaking. Trying to scream his name and barely managing to make a feeble whisper. "Riggins."

"I'm here, Haley. I'm here. Hang on. Help's coming. Just hang on."

Hang on? To what? Why?

He gently brushed the hair out of my eyes. In the narrow tunnel of my vision I saw his fingers. They were sticky with blood. Why was he bleeding?

"I love you." He sounded desperate for me to know. "You'll be all right. Don't let go of the baby. Just don't let go."

"I won't," I whispered, wondering, *What baby?*

The tunnel narrowed to a pinpoint. My world went dark.

Riggins

I cradled Haley in my arms, trying not to move her as my father disappeared into the dark.

I waved my flashlight around. "Here!" I yelled as the security guard came into the tower.

"Help!" I yelled at him. "Call 999! She needs a doctor."

The guard flipped on the light. He paled when he saw the duchess lying fragile and motionless in my arms, blood dripping down her head, a pool of her blood beside us.

"She fell down the stairs. She hit her head badly." I stroked her hair and whispered to her.

It seemed to take forever for medics to arrive. When they did, they took one look at Haley and ordered a medical evacuation helicopter to take her to London.

I walked next to the stretcher, holding her limp hand on the way past the castle to the copter.

"What's going on?" Sid stood on the driveway, being restrained by a policeman. "That's my sister. Let me by. Hale? Haley! Riggins?"

The entire staff was outside on the steps and spilling into the circular drive, watching the helicopter as it waited on the open lawn.

Gibson put his hand on Sid's shoulder. Bird and his son were there. Bird was staring at Sid, looking like he was seeing a ghost.

I didn't have time to stop. I was going in the copter with Haley. "She fell, Sid. She's hurt. We're taking her to a hospital in London. I'll text you the address. Get a car to drive you and meet me there."

Bird stepped forward. "No need, sir. We'll drive her. My son and I will take her." He shot Sid a look of what could only be described as fatherly concern.

Haley

It was all just impressions. The sensation of flying. Light shining through closed lids. Voices, some of them talking to me. Imploring me. Begging me.

I didn't want to open my eyes. I didn't want to see or hear or talk. The pain was too great.

There was something they were afraid of. There was something I was afraid of. But I couldn't remember what. I didn't want to. I wasn't strong enough. I *couldn't*.

Something bad had happened. Something terrible. I couldn't feel my body. I felt separate and distinct from it. I wanted to sleep, just sleep.

Riggins

I stood in the fanatically bright lights of the hospital waiting room and prayed through the long hours while we waited. Prayed like I never had before until Haley's neurosurgeon appeared and called me back to talk to me. Dr. Brace was reportedly the best neurosurgeon in London. I had to trust that was true.

"Is my wife awake? Can I see her?" I walked briskly to keep up with her.

The doctor was kind and friendly, reassuringly arrogant about her skill. "The duchess is sedated, sir. But considering the severity of her fall, the duchess is in good condition. Despite the trauma and the fear of internal skull fractures, the CT scan showed no major surgical lesion."

I barely understood more than her confident tone. I gathered a lack of surgical lesion was a good thing. Why couldn't doctors speak English? Especially here, where the language was born?

"The baby?" My heart pounded wildly. Suddenly I desperately wanted the little interloper. If the baby died, I'd never forgive myself for not wanting my child from the beginning. And Haley would be heartbroken.

"I'll explain more in private." The doctor took me to her office.

I was vaguely aware of pictures of her family. Prints of birds and gardens on the wall that were probably meant to be calming. The usual medical posters. Many of them detailing all kinds of neurological traumas, which were not as reassuring.

"Your wife has had quite the bang to her head," the doctor said, pulling up the CT scan. "There's a hairline fracture. Here." She pointed. "If we can get the swell-

ing down, it should heal without surgical intervention.
She was lucky, very lucky."

I imagined Dr. Brace thinking and adding, *Not to
have cracked her head wide open.*

I shuddered at the imagery that crossed my mind. I
had expected to find Haley broken and cracked. Seeing
her head lying in a pool of blood was bad enough. I
should have breathed a sigh of relief, but there was
more. I could feel it.

"We have her on an IV and medications to relieve
the swelling in her brain."

"Swelling in her brain?" I took a deep breath.

"I'm afraid so. As these things go, it's mild. But it is
causing her to remain in a comatose state."

I must have paled. I felt very cold.

The doctor gave me a reassuring smile. "I believe
the medications should correct it. But brains are tricky
creatures and impossible to predict. But, again, the
swelling isn't severe.

"She's sedated to reduce the pain of her broken arm
and the other trauma from her fall. And prevent her
moving around if she regains consciousness suddenly.
The head of her bed is elevated to aid fluid drainage
from the brain.

"The good news is that despite what you perceived
as a large blood loss, she didn't present with either hy-
poxia or hypotension..."

She kept talking, giving me medical terms. I asked
questions that I hoped made some sort of sense. I was
operating purely on autopilot.

"We set her broken arm."

I nodded. "She was trying to protect the baby as she fell." I had explained how she'd tripped.

The doctor nodded. "She's bruised and has a few cracked ribs. But no other internal damage that we can see."

I hated to ask the next question. "Will she have any long-term damage?"

The doctor gave me a kindly look. "Time will tell."

"When will she wake up?" This was the question we'd been dancing around.

"When she's ready." Dr. Brace patted my hand efficiently.

"The baby?" I took a deep breath. "It's alive, but is it—"

"The baby's beautiful," the doctor said. "Absolutely perfect and healthy. Moving and kicking. It's in no danger. We did an ultrasound. I recorded it if you'd like to see it before I take you to your wife?"

I nodded.

"We know the sex," she said as she brought up the ultrasound on a computer. "Would you like to know what you're having?"

I hesitated only a second. Would it make a difference if I knew? Would it change my mind about anything?

I nodded. "Yes, thank you. I'd like to know."

Haley

I saw nothing but the images my mind created. Dreams or visions; I wasn't sure what they were. I couldn't move. Or maybe I just didn't move. It was hard to tell.

I was wrapped beneath heated blankets, but at times I was chilled to the bone. Weary and wanting to give up. Lights shone through my eyelids. There was beeping and the sounds of machines. That was as close as I got to consciousness before I retreated into the darkness.

The images that swirled through my mind were dark. A handsome man, an older version of someone important, but I couldn't remember who. Pain. A stone staircase. A ghost, a ghost, a ghost. A castle. The end of something. Something chasing me. Someone dead. Someone else I didn't want to lose.

Something I urgently had to hide. It was too late.

I wanted my mom. I called out for her, but my lips didn't move. I screamed for her, but no sound came out. Then I remembered, I was grown and she was dead. And I was all alone.

Sid! Where was Sid? Who was taking care of her?

Sometimes I thought I heard her voice, all grown up and trying to coax me back. And then she faded away.

I was all alone again. Everything was up to me. I had an overwhelming fear of loss.

Someone was holding my hand, squeezing it, kissing it with warm lips. Pressing my hand to wet cheeks. Calling my name. Calling me back. Telling me he loved me. Begging me to come back to him.

I didn't want to come back. I wanted to stay where it was safe and I didn't hurt.

I felt a tiny fluttering as soft as a butterfly in my abdomen. A happy, effervescent feeling, like bubbles in champagne tickling your nose. But this was in my body. Not in my stomach. In my womb. I was still growing a life. Everything was going to be all right. I hoped. All I really knew was that this bubbly little thing needed me. I had to come back for it.

I remembered who I needed. And, more importantly, wanted. I had to fight the darkness. I had to come back. I *wanted* to come back. His name formed on my lips.

Riggins. Riggins. "*Riggins.*"

I was shouting, screaming for him. Despite all my effort, the words came out a bare whisper, just wisps of words amid the electronic beeps in the room. My eyelids felt heavy as I struggled against the weight keeping them down. At last, my eyes fluttered open.

"Haley?" Miraculously, he was there, sitting next to my bed with worry and wonder on his face.

I hadn't dreamed him.

A look of relief crossed his face. Tears stood in his eyes as he smiled through them at me. "You're back."

I nodded, squinting against the light in the room. I'd been in darkness for what seemed like forever. Still holding my hand like he'd never let go, he reached up and dimmed the light by my bed.

"You called me back. I had to come." My throat was dry and scratchy. It was hard to speak. My left arm didn't move, but the right one seemed to work. The rest of my body was sore and bruised.

The baby! I pulled my hand free from his and felt for the baby bump, hoping I hadn't imagined those bubbles.

Still there.

Riggins covered my hand with his over my bump. A small kick from inside brought tears to my eyes.

"It's been active while you were sleeping," Riggins said softly. "You scared the shit out of me, duchess. You've been out three days."

I relaxed, but only somewhat, and smiled, shakily, almost afraid to ask. "The baby? Is it—"

"Perfect. Waiting for you to come to." He squeezed my hand. "It hasn't been sleeping. Much, anyway." He paused. "You fell down the stairs. Do you remember what happened?"

I frowned, trying hard to remember something. Most of it was a blank. "I remember tripping. And falling." I paused. "And then...nothing. Until now."

He nodded. "That's not surprising. You banged your head pretty badly at the bottom of the stone stairs in the Ghost Tower. It was a miracle you didn't crack your skull."

"Thank goodness for hard heads," I said, but it really wasn't funny.

He smiled softly. "You broke your left arm. You wrapped it around your abdomen as you fell. You were trying to protect the baby." He paused again like he was trying to compose himself. "Thankfully, that's the extent of your main injuries. Otherwise, you're just bruised and banged up. Your doctor says the break in the arm is a pretty simple break and should heal without any lasting effects. You'll soon be back to normal."

Memories were coming back in snatches. There was something...something else that was worrying me...

My thoughts were clearing slowly. "Your father?"

Riggins squeezed my hand. "Still dead. As far as anyone but us knows."

He leaned close until we were eye to eye. "I had to make a deal with the devil, but I'm still the duke." He kissed me lightly. "Want to know a secret?"

"More secrets?" I raised an eyebrow.

He grinned. "I know the sex of our baby."

"What?"

He nodded. "They did an ultrasound while you were out. I got to see all ten fingers and ten toes."

"No fair." I paused, waiting for him to fill in the blank. "Are you going to tell me what we're having?"

He shook his head. "Not on your life. We're going to throw that grand gender-reveal party. You'll find out then. Along with everyone else."

I tried to judge from his face. But he was inscrutable. "But I'm the mother—"

He nodded. "Yes, true. But I'm the duke. And fair is fair. You want a girl to inherit the dukedom. Then I think it's high time a father got to tell the mother what they're having.

"I want to surprise you with the grandest gender-reveal party ever. And see the look on your face when you find out boy or girl." His Adam's apple bobbed. "It's an incentive. Something to keep you going. Something to shoot for. Get well and get out of here. Come home. Okay?"

What could I say? Although it was frustrating, it was also sweet and touching. I smiled back at him and nodded.

"Sid's here at the hospital. She'll kill me if I don't call her immediately. She'll want to see you. She has something to tell you and someone she wants you to meet. And I'm sure the doctors will want their turn."

He leaned his forehead against mine. "But first, I have to tell you how ardently I love and admire you."

"Ardently, do you?" I teased, and relaxed against my pillow.

"Desperately. Tragically. Ceaselessly." He took a deep breath and squeezed my hand. "I was a fool not to realize it sooner."

I squeezed his hand in return.

"I can't imagine life without you. Or the baby. Almost losing it..." His voice broke. "Tell me we can raise this baby together, Haley. I'll do anything—"

I put a finger to his lips. "Yes, duke. Of course we'll raise this little lord or lady together. I've been waiting for you to realize the only way we'll ever be happy is together."

Riggins texted Sid, but I didn't get to see her until my doctor examined me and proclaimed my recovery "Brilliant!"

"Just for a minute," Dr. Brace warned. "We can't have her tiring you out. You need your rest." She motioned to the nurse who was assisting.

A minute later, Sid poked her head in the room. "Finally, you're awake, lazy bones!"

"Lazy bones?" I propped myself up on my pillows.

"What else do you call someone who's been in bed for days?" She grinned.

"Are you going to lurk in that doorway forever?" I shook my head. I was tiring. "I thought I taught you better."

She laughed and came over to me, bending down to hug me. "I'm so glad you're back. You gave us a scare! We've all been terribly worried about you." She looked suddenly hesitant, but her eyes burned with excitement. "I hope you don't mind. I brought someone with me. He's in the hall, waiting for a signal that he can come in."

"Don't tell me you've met some handsome Brit and eloped while I've been out," I teased, knowing full well whom she wanted me to meet. I relaxed against my pillow.

She just grinned.

"I'm fading fast." I grinned. "I want to meet him too. Call him before I fall asleep on you both."

She jumped up and went to the door, motioning to someone in the hall. A tall, blond young man stepped inside. I recognized him immediately from his pictures as Bird's son Will. She took his arm and brought him to my bedside.

"Hale, meet my brother Will." She beamed.

I smiled back. But it sounded so odd to hear her say "my" brother. *She* had a brother. And I didn't. I felt that pang of jealousy again.

"Nice to meet you, Will." My voice was still scratchy and soft with emotion.

He hung back slightly.

"Will, meet my sister Haley, the Duchess of Witham." Sid laughed and pulled him forward. "Don't let her title scare you off. She doesn't bite. She's really just a regular person and the best big sister in the world. She only married and became duchess to save me." She winked at me again and laughed. "Isn't this fun? Savior, meet cure!" She bumped Will playfully.

My gaze bounced between them. They looked almost less alike than Sid and I did. At least Sid and I had the same accent and mannerisms. I took pleasure in that.

"Cure?" I said. "Are you sure?"

Sid nodded. "We're being tested to be double sure. But yes, we're pretty confident. And so are our doctors."

The whole story tumbled out, with Sid, and Will, who was amazingly smart and funny like Sid, fighting to tell me all the details.

The night at the Ghost Tower, more than one ghost came to life. Sid came running from the castle at the same time as Bird and Will came from the cottage. When they met in the driveway, Bird took one look at Sid and thought he'd seen the ghost of his half-Chinese, half-white mistress. Until he put two and two together and realized he was really looking into the eyes of his twin daughter.

Thorne had been right about what he'd overheard—Sid *did* have a twin! I was so relieved I could have collapsed. Luckily, I was already in bed.

Bird had hugged Sid, accepted her immediately, and broken down in tears to think of all he'd missed with her and how happy he was to have a daughter. When Thorne realized they'd met and pieced together their relationship, he'd released the "cure" from the Dead Duke—the DNA results and details of their births and adoptions that proved they were full brother and sister.

"You're willing to donate your marrow to save Sid?" I asked Will directly, not caring if I put him on the spot. I meant to. He'd better be willing.

He grinned at her affectionately. "Absolutely. Look at her! I have a beautiful American sister," he said in his gorgeous British accent.

He put his hand to his mouth in an aside to me. "She has to have hot friends she can introduce me to, right?" He gave me two thumbs up and winked. He was completely adorable. "Besides, how many times does a bloke get a chance to save a life? That's something, *really* something. I'm gobsmacked I get to do it."

CHAPTER FOURTEEN

Haley

As I got ready for my gender-reveal party a few
weeks later, I realized that I did believe in fair-
ytales. I really *did*. After all, I was living one, a beautiful one with a happy ending. In as much as real life has
happy endings, anyway.

While I recovered, Sid, Will, and I became close. I
called Will my adopted little brother. He called me
Duchess Big Sis.

Bird told Sid that her mother was the only woman
he'd ever truly loved. And related the whole grand story of his love affair in China. Sid told me he seemed
relieved and happy to finally share it with someone and
get the truth out.

Riggins and I had originally privately worried about how, once the novelty wore off, Will would adapt to finding out that Bird's late wife wasn't his mother. That he was a quarter Chinese. That he had a sister. Who was beautiful and sweet and looked exotically like the Chinese/white mix she was. But Will rolled with it, seemingly delighted and amused by all of it.

He claimed he'd always felt like a part of him was missing, and now that he'd found his twin he was whole. Bird said that when Will was little, he'd had an imaginary friend. A girl with dark hair who Will had claimed was also his twin. Bird had dismissed it as pure fancy then. It broke his heart to think he hadn't paid more attention.

Because of the rarity of a set of twins who looked like two different races, and Rose proclaiming it to the world, and playing up her close connection to them (she was such a media whore), Will and Sid were an immediate sensation.

The very best part was that Will was, indeed, a perfect bone marrow match to Sid. The surgery was already scheduled. Everything I'd done for Sid was now completely worth it.

The whole story of why Sid's mother had left her at an orphanage and how the Dead Duke had found her and arranged for her to be adopted by us was still a bit of a mystery. Since Bird had never known Sid existed, we might never know all of the story.

Only the Dead Duke had known the particulars. I'd been unable to find any records he'd left behind. He was such a methodical, organized, specifically intentioned man that if he hadn't left something behind for me, either he hadn't wanted me to know or felt the details were unimportant.

I privately suspected that the late Mrs. Bird had known something and had refused to accept a Chinese-looking daughter. She wouldn't have been able to pass Sid off as her biological child so she didn't want her. And Sid's mother probably had few choices but to abandon her.

My great-grandfather had, in reality, been a kind man to take care of Bird's child and place her in our loving home. Whether he'd intended to use her as a pawn later, I could only speculate. As I'd thought before, there was no way of knowing she'd develop the anemia in her teens. Without that crucial illness, he would have had no control over me.

As it was, with Sid's cure in hand, my great-grandfather, the Dead Duke, had nothing to hold over me any more. I could walk away from my crazy marriage now. But I wouldn't. Of course I wouldn't. I was madly in love with my duke and his castle. It was even better now that the castle was as much part of Sid's heritage as it was mine.

Sid and Riggins had carried on, planning the gender-reveal party while I recovered. Which was how I found myself standing beneath a beautiful white marquee with a cake cutter in my hand. Before me was the most elaborate ten-tiered cake I had ever seen. It was covered in handcrafted gum paste flowers in blue, pink, and white. Flowers in varieties that we grew on the estate. And the ducal crest tied with blue and pink ribbons.

Riggins stood next to me.

"Judging from the crowd, it looks like the entire village, and half of London, turned out." I took a deep breath.

He nodded and whispered in my ear, "It's a big deal to them. Rose and your PR team did a great job of getting the media to turn out."

"I'm so nervous, I'm shaking." I smiled at him. "In any case, no matter the outcome, it *is* a good human interest story. I must be the only expectant mom in history who doesn't know the sex of her baby before anyone else and has to find out at her own gender-reveal party." I bumped him with my shoulder. "I can't believe you've known since the accident and wouldn't tell me."

"It's more fun this way." His eyes twinkled.

"You would say that."

"I love you," he whispered. "You promised me, boy or girl, we stay together."

"Absolutely. There's no way I'm reneging." I kissed him lightly. "Do you think I'd give up my dukedom?"

He laughed.

"Stop snogging and cut the cake!" someone yelled.

"You heard your people." Riggins covered my good hand with his warm, steady one. "All right. All right! Here we go!"

A dozen or more cameramen gathered in front of us, poised to snap a picture of us cutting the cake. If the color of the cake was pink, we were having a girl. Blue, a boy.

"Ready?" Riggins whispered to me.

I nodded.

"On the count of three!" he yelled.

The crowd began counting. "One. Two. Three!"

We slid the cake cutter into the cake, cut a thick slice, pulled it out, and flipped it onto a plate for everyone to see as cameras flashed around us.

"Blue!" Riggins held the slice out to the crowd. "We're having a boy! We have an heir!"

The crowd erupted in applause. I felt like my knees might buckle.

Riggins took my good arm to steady me. The other one was still in a cast. Tears filled my eyes.

"Surprised?" he asked.

"The blue crumbs gave it away as we cut in."

He pulled me into his arms and kissed me as a shower of blue balloons and confetti rained down around us. Servers took over cutting the cake. A group of young people began passing out blue flowers to all the women in attendance. A band began playing.

TV monitors had been strategically placed around the tent. They now showed the ultrasound of our baby with his boy bits highlighted and circled.

"He's going to hate you for that when he's grown," I said to Riggins.

He shrugged. "He'll probably hate me for a lot of things. That's part of being father and son."

Which I hoped meant he'd forgiven his father, at least a little. Riggins had said that his father had gone back to South America, where he spent most of his time when he wasn't haunting our tower. But there was a part of me that wondered if he was really still lurking around the grounds, watching the festivities and smiling over having a grandson.

Riggins pulled me into his arms and kissed me thoroughly as I rested my hand over our baby.

Gina Robinson is the award-winning author of the romantic comedy Switched at Marriage serial, contemporary new adult romances *Rushed, Crushed, Hushed, Reckless Longing, Reckless Secrets,* and *Reckless Together* and the Agent Ex series of humorous romantic suspense novels. She's currently working on the next Jet City Billionaire romance.

Connect with Gina Online:

My Website: http://www.ginarobinson.com/
Twitter: @ginamrobinson
Facebook: www.facebook.com/GinaRobinsonAuthor